TO PAY
THE PIPER

By

Ileata Kenley

We are fascinated by the darkness in ourselves, we are fascinated by the shadow, we are fascinated by the Boogeyman.

Sir Anthony Hopkins

Table of Contents

Chapter 1

Why Do We Talk to the Dead, If We Are Not Going to Believe Them?

In July of 2017, my family and I had booked an overnight investigation stay at the Malvern Manor in Malvern, Mills County, Iowa. And as always I like to check the history of the location. The Manor is this shabby, yet impressive old hotel. When you drive up and first see the building you are immediately thinking, "Okay yeah, that building has some stories."

The Manor was first opened by Mrs. Julia Betts. In 1890, she purchased the I.B. Ringland home, which had been the heart of Malvern since 1870 and also had once served as the Silver Urn Masonic lodge. She combined it with a warehouse building that was located close to Ringland home and named the new building, "The Cottage Hotel" which served the traveling public for over 50 years. The old hotel has had its share of owners, some good and some not so good and has accommodated a host of interesting characters from doctors, magnetic healers, clairvoyants and traveling snake oil salesmen renting rooms and apartments for many decades, some who perhaps have left a residual imprint.

One night, I had watched the cable program "Paranormal Lockdown", and in this episode Nick Groff and Katrina Weidman were at the Malvern Manor and Johnny Houser was a guest on the show. He claimed to have experienced a not so friendly encounter with a spirit at the Manor. Johnny Houser also happens to be the caretaker of the Villisca Axe Murder House in neighboring Villisca, Iowa. This piqued curiosity; I don't personally know Johnny, but I couldn't imagine why a spirit would be aggressive towards him at Malvern Manor.

What I knew about the Villisca Axe Murder case was limited to what you read on the Villisca Axe Murder House website or hear on the late night podcasts. Eight people were slaughtered, six of the Moore family parents Josiah age 43, Sarah age 39 and children, Herman age 11, Katherine age 9, Boyd 7, Paul age 5 and two of the Stillinger children, Lena age 11 and Ina age 8, who were friends of the family and were invited to sleep over that night. The murders happened in the early morning hours of June 10th, 1912. What I and most people find heartbreaking is the six children, I have grandchildren that age and I cringe just thinking about it. It is an unsolved murder that possibly is connected to similar railroad town killings that terrorized the Midwest and Pacific Northwest communities in 1911-12.

In 1994, the J.B. Moore home in Villisca was completely restored back to the period of 1912, by Darwin Linn and his wife Martha. It is listed on the National Register of Historic Places. The owners offer day tours and nighttime paranormal investigations. I have yet to go, but I will.

Synergy Paranormal from Harvard, Nebraska, had investigated there before I had joined the group in January of 2012, they caught some good evidence from EVP recordings of children's voices and a very clear response from a man with an Irish/British accent answering, "On a Wednesday" to the question of, "When did you die?" So, we all thought it must have been the Reverend George Kelly, a creepy traveling preacher who originally was from England. He was also one of the main suspects of the Moore family murders. Since then I have found out that J.B. Moore's father, Charles C. Moore was born Monaghan, Ireland in 1832. He died in Villisca on a Wednesday, January 29th, 1913.

EVP stands for Electronic Voice Phenomenon. It is the belief that a voice or sounds of a deceased individual can be imprinted on an analog/digital recording device. These are voices/sounds not usually heard by the human ear at the time of the recording but heard upon playback of the device. Some researchers theorize that EVP is caused by the subconscious of a living individual, or "auditory pareidolia", meaning the brain interprets incorrectly what is being heard. But in all honesty, I've experienced/researched Paranormal phenomena as a hobby for 30 plus years, and I just don't think that is the cause in all cases. I do believe we are contacting the spirit world.

So, I decided to find out, as a part of my research into the history of the owners, if there was a connection to the Villisca Axe Murders and the Malvern Manor. They had one particular person with ties to both places, and that was Ralph Piper, one of the four Piper brothers and he had owned the Piper Hotel in the 1940s (Malvern Manor).

First thing I did was to check if the Piper brothers could even be remotely connected to the Villisca Axe Murders of that June night in 1912. I learn enough information to leave me wondering WHY the Piper brothers didn't draw suspicion from the investigating officials at the time of the murders? I also increasingly felt something was a bit fishy with the people connected to the Pipers.

Soon, July 2nd came along it was the day my family and I were to investigate Malvern Manor. It is 175 miles from Hastings, Nebraska, about a four-hour trip. We were meeting my daughter Re'Ana and her husband Carl from Mt. Pleasant, Iowa, at Malvern. My husband and I had bought a new camera set up before the trip, and I was more than thankful my son-in-law, who's an electrician by trade was coming to set it all up. Carl and my husband Kurt are the skeptics, and Carl has Harry Houdini like instincts for debunking. If there is a trick involved, he will find it.

During our investigation, we didn't have a lot of video evidence, other than about a 10-minute stretch in the upstairs room they call Inez's room. My son Chad, Carl and I had left the room about 15 minutes prior to the event, we caught on camera what looked to be a mist that moved back-n-forth in the room and seemed to be checking all the little trinket items in the room that had been left by other investigators. We joked that it was making sure all its treasure was still there after we left the room. We also caught a dark shadow that seemed to move against the back wall, and I have no explanation for it other than it was strange; what is important is that we had a good time as a family. My daughter woke up in the middle of the night to music, which she described as the sounds of

1930's Swing. Sadly, a lot of the audio recording from that night was contaminated by fireworks going off for hours and this strange cat who I'm not kidding yowled outside the kitchen door of the Manor for over an hour. We even tried to bribe the kitty with food but it was not having any part of that! Josh Heard was nice enough to let us bring our old cattle dog Ivan with us on the investigation and I'm sure if we had let the kitty in the Manor, it would have been a bit hard to explain. I'll just leave it at that.

During the night I did feel that Ralph Piper and Cuba Cox, his girlfriend/hotel manager, were still in the old hotel. Ralph gives an "In your Face" type of energy impression letting you know this is *his* Piper hotel and Cuba more of a motherly, softer type energy. She likes the kitchen area of the manor, which only makes sense, as she had operated the restaurant next to the hotel for years.

Close to the end of the night, we were downstairs in what I felt must have been Ralph's area of the hotel. We sat down, and I asked Ralph Piper, "Did your brothers kill the Moore family in Villisca?"

Hoping for a response, I did receive a single reply, "Yes," in a firm tone.

Previously I had watched an episode of "The Dead Files" that featured the Villisca Axe Murder house and Johnny Hauser's home, which is located next door. I found it interesting that Amy Allen who is a Psychic Medium encountered more than one killer on her walk and what she had picked up on, was the Moore family murder was over a business deal. She also said Josiah's wife Sarah, and the Stillinger girls knew the men that attacked them. Amy's partner Steve DiSchiavi who is a retired police detective disagreed with her over the known evidence he had been provided. Based on the information, he favored the insane Reverend George Kelly as the killer. I admire Amy Allen, I follow her on Twitter, and I tend to believe her.

So, thanks to Ralph's EVP, I have joined the countless others who have pulled their hair out trying to determine once and for all who killed the Moore family on June 10th, 1912, in Villisca. I'm confident I have found them. I have included a lot of newspapers, dates and page numbers, if you want to follow along and decide for yourself.

My story, which is Ralph's story focuses on the lives of the Piper brothers, the years leading up to and the suspicious activity around the time the Moore's were murdered and afterwards. I decided to approach this monster mystery case as if the Piper Brothers could have been the two killers that fateful night and in the process possibly discovering Col. E.B. Piper's dark secret.

Chapter 2

The Piper Family Of Monroe County, Iowa

In this second chapter, I want to explain who the Pipers were and give some possible insight into what factors could have turned these brothers into killers.

William and Margaret Piper moved to Monroe County, Iowa in 1846. They had six children, Sophia, Nathan, William, Dudley, Elizabeth, and Leonidas. The three eldest children were born in Virginia before moving to Iowa. The Piper family had moved west from Washington County, Virginia which is part of the Blue Ridge Highland area of the Appalachian Mountains. On the 1830 Federal census for Washington County, Virginia, the Pipers are listed as farmers.

An important event in Virginia's history happened in August 1831. Nat Turner who was an educated minister and a slave would inspire a rebellion among fellow slaves which started in Southampton County, Virginia. Whole families of white farmers, as many as 60 men, women and children were murdered in their beds as they slept, by a small band of the hatchet-wielding slaves. The aftermath saw horrible consequences for African Americans living in the area whether they were involved or not. It sent terror throughout Virginia and later the entire South and fueled the fires of some of the events that eventually led up to the American Civil War.

Some of the early settlers who came to that part of Monroe County, Iowa were part of the "Hairy Nation". The name comes from the local Native Americans' accounts of the appearance of the Appalachian and Frontier settlers (Mountain People). In fact, the first white child born in the county was in 1820. These settlers were mainly of Irish and Scotch ancestry; they also were divided into family clans. Their favorite pastime was drinking whiskey and fighting with anybody. There is an account from the Illustrated History of Monroe County Iowa, where the local Clans would go to Albia and fight with each other using axe handles. The "Nation" didn't seem to like the Northeasterners who were religious, prohibitionist and abolitionists. In the early years, there appears to have been a lot of conflict among the different groups.

There were also the coal miners who came in the 1870s from Wales who settled in the coal camps in Monroe County and others from the coal mining states of Virginia, Kentucky, and Tennessee seeking a new life after the Civil War. In 1879, there was a miner strike and the Consolidated Coal Company sent men to Virginia to hire African American strikebreakers. By 1880, 90% of the workers were African American and 10% European immigrants, mostly Bohemians, who created the town of Buxton. It was one of the first truly racially integrated communities with little to no segregation or racial discrimination. But outside of Buxton, this didn't settle well with people. The original miners in the area who suddenly had no jobs and families to feed; there were several violent encounters. The Piper family were the auctioneers for most of the sheriff sales in Monroe County. So, one would assume they would know how to defend themselves. In 1881, the Consolidated Coal Company was bought by the Chicago & North Western (C&NW) Railroad, and by 1919, the population of Buxton had dwindled from a high of 7,000 to a mere 400 citizens.

The Pipers were lifelong Democrats even though they supported the Union in the Civil War. The older generation remained Democrats after the war. They very much stuck with their Southern views and often had tongue and cheek newspaper fights with Republicans over politics. Edward and Will Piper became Republicans and Edward later switched back to the Democrat party when he ran for Congress in 1922.

1863 Monroe County Militia Roll

Piper, Charles J. 19, Farmer. Monroe

Piper L. K. 18,, Farmer. Troy

Piper, N. C. 32, Farmer. Albia

Piper, W. R. 25, Farmer. Troy

Piper William J. 21 Farmer Monroe

The Piper family also made the newspapers regularly.

A few articles stood out:

Frank Piper was in trouble in 1897, for making whiskey on the old miner property in Albia.

In 1898, the State of Iowa vs. Harry Piper for assault with intent to commit great bodily injury, but it was ignored by the grand jury.

In 1901, James Piper apparently went into a scuffle with the night man at the Albia train depot over refusing to give the conductor a ticket to ride the train. This fight was not the first one James had with the railroad employees. James died a couple of years later and apparently they had to roll a drunken man out of the way so his funeral procession could pass (*The Albia Republican*, June 2nd, 1904, pg1). It's obvious some of the Pipers inherited love for Appalachian Mountain Moonshine and fighting!

Leonidas (Lon) K. Piper was the father of the brothers of my story. Leonidas and Grace Piper from Albia, Iowa had four sons and one daughter, Edward Boyd Piper (E.B. Piper), William Harrison Piper (W.H. Piper), Albert Chase Piper (A.C. Piper), Ralph Knox Piper (R.K. Piper), and Ida May Piper (Dodd).

The Lon Piper family were auctioneers, debt collectors and had operated an auction firm in Albia for thirty years, and then later in Corning. The senior Piper, Lon K., seemed to be a well-respected man in Adams and Monroe County, Iowa. He ran for sheriff as a Democrat in 1893 in Monroe County, he lost that election but did hold office as councilman in Urbana Township for years. His brother Nat Piper, a local merchant in Albia also was involved in local politics. His eldest son Edward joined him as a full partner in the auction business in 1896. Lon K. Piper would die in 1901 crying a sale in Corning, and strangely the two brothers would use that for a 'motto" in some of their weekly upcoming Auction newspaper ads.

Edward Boyd Piper

Ed or (E.B.) is the eldest son of Lon and Grace. From a young age, he was working with his father in the auction business; in fact, he cried his first sale at age 13. In the fall of 1894, Ed enrolled in college in Humeston, Iowa. Years later, his mother Gracie would reminisce about making his suit for the first day of college, how she stained the material with walnut shells that she used to make the suit herself. Ed was a brilliant student and he soon graduated at a young age and immediately went on to teach school at the White schoolhouse in Mantua Township, 1895. Edward accepted the position as Principal of the school at Mt. Etna, Iowa in 1896, an impressive feat at age 19 years! During his first year as Principal, the students receiving a diploma in 1897 were Sadie and Emma Sink, Cora Bell Sterns, Peal Southwick, Daily Johnson, Rachel Roberts, May Finkel, Myrta Reed, Sarah Hollingsworth, Willie Hickox and Cleveland Coakley. It was announced that Miss Stella Strawback would now teach the younger students and Ed would teach the older students. Then later the same year it was announced that he would now teach in Creston, Iowa. It was obvious there was a problem with Edward, or he would not be moving around to schools. Also, keep the name Hollingsworth in mind; it will come up later in the story in connection with a train axe murder in Illinois. On August 13th, 1898, he married Miss Cora Sterns, one of his past students. By 1899, he had given up or was encouraged to give up on his teaching ambitions and was full time working with his father as an auctioneer and partner in the family business.

On April 4th, 1900, Edward and Cora's only child was born Carl Wesley Piper. The same month Ed went into business with Charles E. Okey to sell farm implements as the manager in Corning. Later that year on November 9th, there was a big fire in the city of Corning starting at the livery stable that destroyed the Piper, and Okey implements warehouse. The two men decided to sell out and auction the remaining stock later that month, and Edward's father L.K. Piper cried the sale for them. Edward was now going by Col. E.B. Piper; the title of Colonel was given to auctioneers and was a tradition that dated back to the Civil War. Only the Colonel was allowed to auction war bounty. He had 38 sales dated ahead in Iowa, Nebraska, and Missouri and he was a very successful auctioneer. In June 1901, his father Lon passed away, and by all accounts in the newspaper, he was a well-liked man. Edward was called home for the wake and burial.

In January 1902, E.B. opened an office as an auctioneer with T.C. Reid, another implement dealer in Corning. In August of '02, his younger brother William (W.H.) Piper joined him in the sale business as an auctioneer, and it was known by Piper Bros, and Will opened a second auction office in Villisca, Iowa that same year. Several Adams County Court cases arose in October of '02. One incident involved Edward and the Smith family over some land documents and another between E.B. and W.H. Piper, and a court ordered a guardian was appointed. I'm no legal expert so I'm not sure what all that means other than it seems like Edward had some bad business deals. Edward also had a falling out with the rest of the Piper family over Lon K.'s estate; he filed a lawsuit and won in October 1902. The brothers must have worked out their differences, and they continued as partners. They seemed to be very successful, one news article shows they had sales every day in September that year.

One article in March 1903, *Adams County Free Press* pg.5, was good for a chuckle. A reporter passing by T.C. Reid's place of business was drawn into Edward's voice hustling to sell Mr. Reid's implement stock to a sizable crowd that had gathered to watch the show. He stopped and asked, "Are you going out of business?"

Reid replied "No, Mr. Piper is just helping me out; He is selling my merchandise as if it is an auction." He later would claim it was the best sales day of the year for him.

In 1905, Edward started to sell insurance for New York Life, in addition to the auctioneer business. He traveled all over the Midwest, writing home in a letter to the *Adams County Free Press*, he had sold 39,000 dollars' worth of insurance in one month. As if he didn't have enough irons in the fire already, he also became the manager/coach of the local men's baseball team in Corning.

The year 1909 came along, Edward was now age 32; he had opened a new flashy Buick car dealership in Corning and started to travel the central part of the Country selling cars, in addition to the Piper Bro's auction service. Later that year Edward, his brother Will (W.H.) and fellow Corning resident Matt Gourd traveled to Mexico to scout out the prospects of farmland in that country. He also became a land agent for the country of Mexico and started to make regular trips there to sell land.

Will Harrison Piper

Will (W.H.) was three years younger than his brother Edward and it was clear from the beginning that he had to play second fiddle to his older brother. Ed was the more outgoing and very bombastic. Will was more a loner "cowboy". His father Lon coddled his older brother and took Ed from young age with him to his auctions. From the news articles of the day, one gets the impression that he paraded the boy around like a mascot. Will, on the other hand, worked with his uncle Nat in his merchant store in Albia and on the family farm. He did eventually begin to work sales on the side with his father and brother. At age seventeen, Will traveled to Minnesota by himself on a harvest and threshing crew for a season. The next year in 1898, he went even further west with two others to South Dakota for work and the trio of young men made their way there camping out along the way.

In April of 1903, Will Piper was badly hurt when thrown from a wagon into a tree while on a country ride with his soon to be wife Mary Sterns, the younger sister of Cora B., Edward's wife. His right shoulder was thrown out of place (*Adams County Free Press*, April 8th, 1903).

Will and Mary Sterns were married on the Fourth of July in 1904. Tragically, after just two short years she died of complications from a bout of Diphtheria at her sister Cora B. Piper's home in Corning. Curiously enough, she passed away while Will was in Villisca renting a house. (*Adams County Free Press*, Dec 12th, 1906)

Within four months he married Cora A. Spencer Paulins, the widow of Villisca's blacksmith, John Paulins, who died in August of '06. Cora (Ora) A. was also the daughter of Martin VanBuren Spencer (M.V.), a merchant and judge from Corning, Adams County. I found a picture of her online taken with the Spencer family at age 22, and I was surprised by how tiny she was. She reminded me a lot of the actress Linda Hunt who has hypo-pituitary dwarfism (short stature). Cora and Will never had any children, and she seems to have often been ill. Will always attended events alone and Cora spent close to four months in the summer of 1912 in Excelsior, Missouri for repeated diphtheria attacks. I found it interesting and worth a mention that Cora Spencer was Methodist and a member of the Eastern Star.

In April 1907, Will Piper and his new bride moved to Villisca to a house on West Fourth Street, west of the Opera House (*Adams County Free Press*, April 24th, 1907). The Pipers must have torn down the original house because they built a new two-story house on the corner of Fourth Street and Second Avenue the next year. (*The Villisca Review,* August 13th, 1908)

Will Piper owned the 60 acres adjoining Villisca from the south and in May of 1908, W.H. Piper went to court in Red Oak, the county seat for Montgomery County to ask for a temporary injunction to prevent the city residents from dumping waste and dead animals close to his rental property. His petition was denied. (*The Villisca Review*, May 7th, 1908). In the years before the Moore family murders, there were several complaints from the citizens of Villisca about the area "South of the track." It seems this area served as a favorite camping grounds for hobos, traveling poor and African Americans.

In July 1908, Will Piper traded the 60 acres adjoining Villisca to the south to George Montaldo for four houses in Corning. (*Adams County Free Press,* July 1st, 1908), 1909 was a busy year full of auction dates for the Piper brothers. Almost always the same people were involved, Billie (J.W.) Rose, who served the food, and F.F. Jones or F.L. Ingman were usually the clerks.

Will and his wife Cora set off on one of Edward's trips to Mexico in April along with several other Villisca citizens. All of them said they were not happy with that country; it was too hot and dry. But the trip was worth the money as a sightseeing excursion. (Pg.5, *The Villisca Review*, May 6th, 1909)

One article in December, tells of Will walking 14 miles one day to a sale and another 14 miles the next day to a different sale. Then he walked back to Corning, arriving at his brother Ed's house at 11 p.m., because of the roads being bad. (Pg. 12, *The Villisca Review*, Dec.9th, 1909). I think it is safe to say Will must have been physically fit, not to mention unafraid of wolves or the dark.

Beginning in 1910, Will started to host big horse sales in Villisca. He was the sole manager; it appeared that he and Edward were on the outs again. Later, J.W. (Billie) Rose took over these horse sales, and he continued to be the auctioneer. The business became Piper & Rose Horse Sales. The thought of losing control of Will was what, I think, sent Edward over the edge in 1911, or you could say "blunt side" (sorry, bad joke).

Frank F. Jones must have considered Will trustworthy enough to send him to help his store manager, J.L. Palmquist, to pick up a Brush Runabout car in Omaha for a customer. (Pg. 5, *The Villisca Review*, May 25th, 1911). So, they had some kind of chummy relationship besides odd jobs and the auction business. There is a possibility he also did bank debt collection for the Villisca bank and Jones, but I do not have proof of this, just that his father and brother were debt collectors in Albia and Corning.

Albert Chase Piper, Ida May Piper (Dodd) and Ralph Knox Piper

Albert Chase was born Dec 25th, 1883, and died on April 17th, 1951. He also went by Allie or A.C., and he seems like the "good Piper." There were not many newspaper articles about him, he remained in Monroe County for his whole life and he had three marriages. The first came in 1906, when he married Julia Hollingshead of Albia. Julia's father ran a competing auction service in Albia, which might explain the bitter feelings, or maybe he didn't approve of his brothers' lifestyles. The couple moved to the L.K. Piper homestead located in Urbana Township. Julia died in January 1914, after a short illness. I found it strange that only the wives of the other Piper brothers attended the funeral. There seems to have been a family rift beginning in 1906 between Albert, Edward, and Will, and later would include Ralph. I also noticed in reading Albert's obit in 1951, it made no mention of his brothers or sister or even their families. Albert and Julia belonged to the Brethren church and it is possible their religious differences played a role in the split of this family. Albert married later that year in November of 1914 to Onie V. Fisher. She passed away in 1926, and then he married Nellie (Pearl), who shows up on the 1930 Federal Census as living in Mantua, Monroe County, Iowa.

Ida May Piper (Dodd) was born in February of 1882 (exact date unknown). Ida was teaching school in Albia in 1900. Edward and Ida seem to have been the apple of their parents' eye, and both were teachers. Ida May married Luke Dodd on June 24th, 1908, in Albia. Luke Dodd was from Taylor, Iowa, and he had a possible cousin named Cecil, who becomes important later in the story. Ida Piper, now Dodd, was living with her husband in Fort Morgan, Colorado in 1911. She would often travel back to Iowa to visit family members. She must have thought highly of Ralph, her younger brother, because her eldest son was named Ralph as well and sadly he was killed in an accident near Harris, Missouri in 1939. He was instantly killed by the collapse of a stone crusher as he was loading the hopper. The Dodds had another son born June 23rd, 1912, named Russell E. The last time I find him in the records was in 1940, he was living with his parents in Rocky Boone, Missouri.

Ralph Knox Piper was born April 29th, 1887 and died January 31st, 1949. He was the youngest of the Piper family and naturally, he was a bit of a rebel. Ralph is my favorite in part for his EVP that sent me on this adventure writing this book and besides that, he raced some really cool Excelsior motorbikes. The first newspaper article that mentions him is a proclamation: "Ralph Piper, went to church this morning," that was when he was seventeen. The next you hear of him, Ralph is holding down a claim in South Dakota for the family. On August 10th, 1910, he married Helga Halverson, age 20, in Pierre, South Dakota. She was the daughter of a Norwegian immigrant and a neighbor of Ralph's. The 1910 Federal census has Ralph living in Township 8, Stanley, South Dakota, owning a farm at age 24, but I'm positive this was the Piper land that Ralph was put in charge of several years before. Stanley County is in the center of the state bordering the Missouri River and only in 1907 was the Black Hills region connected to the railroad line, opening this area to settlers. Ralph and Helga had one son, Edward. I will write more about them later.

Chapter 3

The Murder of the Moore Family, Fire at the Farm and Thomas Gill

I had reservations about writing this story; this tragedy has left an enduring wound on the Villisca community and not just at Villisca but people all over the county. Folks are so entrenched in their beliefs on **Who** and the **Why** these murders happened, it's almost as if they feel they **"Own"** the narrative and nothing will ever change their minds. I'm hoping this book will at least introduce a different conversation with new ideas.

I do not think that Paul Mueller is the same man who committed all these axe murder crimes in 1911-1912. He had been suggested as the Villisca murderer in the book by Bill James and his daughter Rachel about Mueller titled "Man from the Train". A really interesting book that did introduce a different conversation, but the only crime that has been associated with Paul Mueller, which it has never been established that is even his real name, happened in January 1898, in Brookfield, Massachusetts; then the man just disappeared. The circumstances are not the same. Mueller, a German immigrant, spoke very poor English and most likely couldn't read it. He also lived and worked for the victims, the motive in that murder was robbery and the home was ransacked, doused with kerosene and the only covering of faces was the female victims whose bed clothes had been pulled up over their heads to expose them from below the waist. Also, the victims were struck in the abdomen and various parts of the body with the axe, not just the head. (*North Adams Transcript,* from North Adams, Massachusetts Jan 10th, 1898, pg. 1) (*North Troy Palladium*, Jan 13th, 1898, pg. 2) In my opinion he would have lacked the intellectual finesse to plan all the intricate details that link these series of crimes together.

I was not familiar with Villisca case to begin with but I am now, and I had only Ralph Piper's one word and well, he is a Ghost! After sitting on Ralph's EVP revelation for about a year, I decided to piece it all together from books, newspaper clippings and going through the mountain of information found online that Dr. Edgar V. Epperly had researched. He spent years preserving the history of this story, if not for him it would have been lost in time otherwise. I listened to the paranormal investigators who visited the Villisca Axe murder house and their EVP recordings, also the Psychic impressions that individuals had.

Many thanks to my daughter Re'ana for the countless hours she spent driving all over Iowa to the Historical Society and various County offices looking up and verifying information for the book, and to the folks who helped her.

The Gettingtheaxe internet blogger Inspector Winship has studied and blogged about the Midwest Axe Murders, although I never quite sold him on the fact that a ghost told me this story. I could not have put this all together without his information about the various axe murders. He also asked me a question that I really needed to be asked, in an email he wrote, "Forget the Paranormal and tell people, Why, should we consider the Pipers a suspect?" The more I thought about his question I ask now, "Why shouldn't we?" More interestingly, "Why didn't the investigators at the time of the murders?" Well, the best I can figure is the Piper Brothers were well known, though it's debatable whether people liked them or not.

We know now from FBI research that a good number of serial killers are upstanding individuals of their community, also they are some of the most evilest, like H.H. Holmes, John Wayne Gacy, Ted Bundy, Richard Angelo, who was an Eagle Scout and Albert Fish, a seemingly nice normal husband and father of six, who secretly raped, killed and ate countless children.

Villisca's Mayor F.L. Ingman often worked with Will Piper on horse sales, which were held at the J.W. Rose horse barn that was located close to the Moore home. So, seeing Col. Will Piper in the area would go unnoticed and not reported, also he had just had a big horse sale on Saturday the 8th. Will Piper also did odd jobs or they were personal favors for Frank F. Jones because he did not "need" money. His brother Edward did debt collecting besides both of them being auctioneers, in which they worked regularly with Frank Jones and his son Albert who were often the clerks for the various sales. When wealthy important people hire a debt collector/contract killer they do not hire a prison convict, they hire a professional and someone who will keep their secret, especially this one.

The Murder

Josiah (Joe) B. Moore, age 43, owned J.B. Moore farm implement and hardware store in downtown Villisca and he and his wife Sarah Montgomery Moore, aged 39, their four children, Herman, age 11, Katherine, 10, Boyd, 7 and Paul, 5, lived in a modest two-story home at 508 E 2nd Street.

June 10th, 1912, it was early morning in Villisca about 5:00, Mrs. Mary Peckham went out to hang her laundry on the line, and she noticed it was eerily quiet at her neighbor's house, the Moores. In 1912, people didn't sleep in late, the four Moore children were not outside yet and there were morning chores to be done. A couple of hours went by and Mrs. Peckham could see there was no activity still from the Moore home and by now the horses and cow were getting impatient and the chickens were fussing to be let out. Mary decided to head over to the Moore's and see what was going on with her neighbors. She knocked on the door, but received no answer, so then she tried the doorknob. The home was locked, and she noticed all the window shades were pulled. It seemed strange to her, most people liked the fresh morning air blowing through their house.

So, Mrs. Peckham went back to her home and phoned Joe Moore's brother Ross, who was a druggist in town. Ross came over and tried the other doors, only to find them all locked also. He took a spare skeleton key from his pocket, and opened the door to pitch blackness -- this was the moment he must have known something was wrong; blood and death have a distinct odor. Ross yelled for his brother or anyone but only silence answered back. He walked across the parlor to the spare bedroom and opened the door to see in the dim light two figures under the bed sheets and some clothes, and he saw dark stains on the wall behind the head of the bed. He immediately returned to the front porch and told Mary Peckham to call the city Marshal, Hank Horton.

Hank Horton showed up with Joe Moore's store employee Ed Selley and the two men proceeded to examine the home. Marshal Horton went through the house and opened the shade on a window. They proceed to the guest room on the ground floor where Lena and Ina were located, but they couldn't identify the girls. After seeing the Stillinger girls' bodies, Selley went outside and waited. He was too ill from the horrific sight or too scared to continue. Horton lit a match and proceeded to goes upstairs where he discovered the bodies of the whole Moore family. He then went downstairs and out onto the front porch where he uttered the memorable quote, "My God, Ross, there is someone murdered in every bed," to Josiah's brother.

The two bodies in the downstairs guest bedroom were later identified to be two sisters, Lena Stillinger, aged 11, and Ina Stillinger, aged 8, who had been invited to spend the night at the Moore house after attending an evening Sunday school program at the local Presbyterian Church.

All had been bludgeoned to death with an axe, all the windows in the house had the shades drawn down and mirrors in the house had been covered with the Moores' clothing. A plate of food was prepared on the kitchen table along with a wash basin full of bloody water.

In the downstairs spare bedroom where the Stillinger girls were found, there was a kerosene lamp at the foot of the bed with the chimney removed. Leaning up against the south wall of the room was Josiah Moore's own axe, that he usually kept outside by the barn for chipping coal. The killer had attempted to wipe it clean but the axe still had blood and hair on it. Next to it was a four pound slab of bacon (in some versions it was two) wrapped in a dish towel, a broken piece of key or a watch's chain was found lying on the floor and Josiah Moore's pocket watch had been moved from upstairs and now was on the dresser in the room. (This might be a folklore, because I have never heard Dr. Epperly talk about his watch). Lena, the older of the two Stillinger girls, even though she was 11 almost 12, was adult size and a woman in many ways. And she was the only one who the investigators thought woke up because she had what appeared to be a defensive wound on her arm. She was pulled down in bed after her death, they know this because her brain matter was still on the pillow and wall behind the headboard and she had been posed by the killer and there was also a blood smear on her inner knee. The coroner determined that none of the female victims had been sexually assaulted. Lena's nightgown had been pulled up above her waist and she had no underwear on, her underwear was used to wipe off the axe and discarded under the bed. I think it is possible that her gown could have hiked up as she was being pulled down in the bed and she took off her own underwear earlier, knowing she would have to wear them again the next day (trust me, it's a woman thing). The posing of her body might have been for shock value or for visual sexual stimulation. Later at the trial of Reverend Kelly, a criminal expert from the Oregon Prisoner Aid Society suggested the slab of bacon found in the bedroom was used as a masturbation aid.

Robbery was not the motive it seems because nothing of value that was noticed by family or investigators had been taken other than Joe Moore's keys seemed to be gone, but the dressers had been gone through, because the killer used the Moore's own clothing to cover mirrors and the door glass.

There was a crime scene examination on Tuesday, the second day after the murder, by M.W. McCaughey, the assistant Warden of Leavenworth Prison in Kansas, who apparently arrived in Villisca in a drunken state. After he sobered up, McCaughey looked for fingerprints but could not find any usable areas to work, as the whole crime scene had be contaminated by crowds of people walking through the home. Bert McCaul even picked up a piece of Josiah Moore's skull for a keepsake and was showing it off at his billiards hall. I'll add the narrative that Josiah Moore had no enemies in Villisca can't be correct because obviously Bert McCaul wouldn't be so comfortable showing off the murdered man's skull as a souvenir if he wasn't in the presence of likeminded company. However, McCaughey suggested that the deep gouges made from the swing of the axe in the parents' room were made by a left-handed individual and in the south bedroom which was the Moore children's, he determined that the killer had to be swinging wildly and over his head one-handed because strangely enough the marks in the children's room were in the center of the room and not above the beds. Both of these rooms are located on the second story of the home along with a small attic space. The small house has a little narrow winding staircase that leads upstairs right into Josiah's and Sarah's bedroom, and there was also a kerosene lamp placed at the foot of their bed with the chimney removed and set aside under the dresser.

The coroner, Dr. Lindquist, who was from Stanton, Iowa, noted that Joe Moore's head was completely gone from the mouth upwards, the top part of his skull had been smashed by the blunt side of the axe multiple times so hard that it was embedded into the mattress and pillow of the bed, and his wife Sarah seemed to be the only one hit with the blade side of the axe at an acute angle and her skull had been turned into multiple one inch wide slices. The coroner also speculated that the killer had first delivered an incapacitating blow to Josiah and Sarah, then the killer returned a second time to decimate the heads of the parents; this is what is called an "Overkill". Sarah's shoes were located on Josiah's side of the bed, blood had dripped into the shoe from the first wounds, enough to fill the shoe and then when the killer had come back to overkill, he kicked over the shoe and then blood dripped onto the sole of the shoe. There was a significant time between the two attacks on the parents. This tells us Joe and Sarah, the parents were probably attacked first and were the primary targets because of the blood in Sarah's shoe, the obvious demonstration of brutal rage in their murders and that the Moore and Stillinger children did not exhibit overkill, they were only struck once or twice, but their heads were not as hard as an adult's head.

I used Dr. Epperly's CSI Iowa interview located on YouTube and as one of the references, I highly recommend it.

As an experiment, I approached a co-worker who works in the trailer bay. Part of his job is to break out the old flooring on heavy hauler trailers, so he swings 3 to 5 pound sledgehammers regularly.

I asked him to swing that hammer 30 times really fast busting boards. I'll add that he is 25 years of age and works out daily at the gym. He was able to do it, but in his opinion the accuracy of hitting a target would suffer after about 10 fast swings, especially in dark or low light, which would naturally disorient a person. In his opinion, whoever committed this crime would have to be a very physically fit individual, or was able to take his time killing the people. I found out what I needed to know, and that is a 120 pound feeble little preacher man did **not** do these killings!

The scenario as I speculate it happened on June 10, 1912

Frank Jones contracted the Piper brothers to murder Josiah Moore in the fall of 1911. I think Vina Tomkins, who was a Grand Jury witness, was probably was telling the truth when she claimed in the fall of 1911, that she overheard three men talking about money by an old slaughterhouse just southeast of Villisca. Vina had told Detective Wilkerson that she thought one of them was Frank F. Jones but when she was in front of a judge, she wouldn't swear to it in court. This old slaughterhouse was where the citizens and merchants of Villisca disposed of wooden crates. In October 1911, there was a Duroc-Jersey Hog sale at Hopkins feed barn in Villisca. (Sept 28th, 1911, *The Villisca Review*, pg. 8) Will Piper was the auctioneer, and F.F. Jones raised register hogs, so this was a sale he would have likely been at or at least Albert, his son. On the sale bill, it said to bring your own crates. (Where do they get the crates, at the old slaughterhouse.) These men often worked auctions together, so if not this particular sale it could have been another.

I don't think F.F. Jones had any idea that the whole family would be murdered. I don't think he was that kind of man, though arrogant and a liar, undoubtedly. I also think there were more individuals who were involved with at least the cover-up of the murders. One article that appeared in 1949, was an interview with an elderly woman named Aunt Molly Robe, who personally knew the Moore family. She said that she used to think the murders were done by an insane person in 1912, but now years later she felt differently. To quote her: "The murders were too well planned and too well covered." (Feb 24th, 1949, *Des Moines Tribune*, pg. 28). I would say the townspeople knew it was a local murder.

I wondered if the Pipers could have been just expecting only Josiah at the house that evening but planned for either scenario, thinking J.B. would be planning a romantic tryst with a lady friend while his wife and children were at the Presbyterian church's children's program. With one of the brothers stuck in the attic waiting, they were forced into plan B mode when the whole family came home together. The problem I have with the only killing Josiah Moore scenario is, it would not have matched the other axe murders and there would be no reason to kill the Hudson couple in a double murder in Paola, Kansas only days before. Where Edward had left specific clues linking the previous murders together implying both murders were done by a traveling axe murderer. Also, I would say there is something more than an affair with a daughter in law and losing a John Deere franchise that generated that kind of hate. Is it possible that Joe Moore or someone in the community was blackmailing Frank F. Jones with an election upcoming? Or was Joe Moore having multiple affairs with the ladies of Villisca?

There had to be two killers that night. I do not think it would be possible to kill eight people in a two-story home without someone waking up and calling for help. The impact alone on the bed is going to cause a response from the other individual sleeping in the same bed and to get away with this multiple times with a neighbor's home less than 30 feet away, not to mention these murders happened in June, and most people would have a window opened for the cool night air. That also means the Moores probably had windows open and we know from the scene of the crime they were all closed, so making sure the 12 windows were all closed would have happened after the murders. The Villisca house is different in that it has two stories, 7 rooms, 12 windows with a small winding creaky staircase, whereas the other Midwest axe murders locations were single story 2 or 3 room cottage dwellings.

I think E.B. Piper and W.H. Piper "staged" the crime scene to look like the other railroad town murders. Ed would read the newspaper stories about the other killings in detail on his train travels, or as I suspect he could have committed some of those Midwest axe murders himself, which kind of leaves me at a dilemma. Has there ever been a serial killer who staged one of his killings for profit? If not, I think Edward Piper might be a first.

Anyway, back to the story. Both men's wives were out of state, leaving Ed staying at Will's farm located one mile north of town. I think Edward probably arrived earlier in Villisca and possibly he is the man spotted going into Moore's home that day, possibly waiting for Josiah and then when the family showed up having to hide in the attic where he smoked a couple of cigarettes waiting for the Moores to go to bed for the night. Will had to be somewhere he could see the east side of the house which is the direction the attic windows face, waiting for a signal to come in the back door later. The whole town was without street lights making it very easy to view a flame from a simple strike of match. I think both men could have worn moccasins, as the Pipers owned property in Sioux territory in South Dakota and Will had just returned from the Piper ranch which is located in Draper, South Dakota, the summer of 1911.

Edward Landers was staying with his mother that summer in Villisca, and she lived a few houses from the Moores. He testified at the Coroner's inquest that he heard "Hooting," like signal calls that boys do, at approximately 11:00 the night of the murders.

They clearly knew the layout of the house, being as they auctioned many properties in the area and that home had a standard floor plan, or they could have even visited the home previously. Edward was left-handed and Will Piper had an old but severe right shoulder injury, which means he most likely would have swung an axe left-handed. The most common motion to lose with a shoulder injury is shoulder flexibility, because the tendons and small muscles in a person's shoulder, even after surgery won't return to full functionality. So, he could have been right-handed but used an axe or hammer left-handed and probably without the best control, so either of the brothers could have been the one who left the marks on the ceiling with the axe. Will Piper according to his WW1 and WW2 draft cards, was of medium build, brown hair and blue eyes. Oddly enough, on the WWII "Old Man's Draft" Registration Card, his height and weight are missing.

One of the most chilling aspects of these murders for me was what Psychic/Medium Amy Allen had said about the Stillinger girl knowing her assailant that night. Will sold Shetland ponies to the parents of the children of Villisca and every time I think of this, I can't help but choke up with my own emotions.

Edward came out of the attic with a pistol butt or baton, striking Josiah and Sarah Moore, knocking them unconscious. Will first killed the Stillinger girls Lena and Ina with the axe he picked up from the backyard, and then he went upstairs and killed the Moore children, Herman, Katherine, Paul, and Boyd, returning to the other room to deliver the finishing blows to the parents. The two brothers then spent a bit of time in the Moore house staging it to look exactly as close to the axe murder reports in the newspapers as they could, even possibly posing the Stillinger girl's body. The bacon slab and preparing of food I think were there more or less to imply a transient had committed the murders. The covering of the windows had to be after the killings, which left me in doubt that the killer or killers did it to have privacy with Lena's body because they could have just shut the bedroom door and only covered the windows in the room where the Stillinger girls were sleeping. I think the Pipers could have possibly been looking for blackmail documents containing information about F.F. Jones.

I think they left the exact route the bloodhounds took. The dogs leaped off the porch heading east and then turned north on South 6th, Avenue. The dogs turned west on East 1st Street, and then paused at the intersection of East 1st Street and North 5th

Street. Frank F. Jones lived in the big yellow Victorian house on the corner. I wonder if the dog didn't pick up a scent for a second. The Senator's home was directly south one mile from Will Piper's farm, but the dogs continued west on East 1st Street, then turned and headed south on 1st Avenue to the edge of town, crossing the tracks and continuing until they reached the West Nodaway River. The bloodhounds repeated this route the next day as well. So, this was the route the killers took. Despite what Hollywood films depict, it is darn near impossible to trick well-trained bloodhounds. The TV program "Myth Busters" tested multiple theories and failed not once but twice. Bloodhounds are an "Air Scent" dog, meaning they track by sniffing the air as well as the ground. Also, going back to the bacon, had either one of them been fiddling with the bacon as some suggest or had been an unwashed traveling vagrant, I'm confident those bloodhounds would have been able to track the killer(s) to the next county and back or at least to the train track. I think the Pipers probably either walked or swam up the river. The reason I think up the river is they would have to go against the river current to avoid the dogs tracking the scent and then it is still hard because the scent drifts in the water along the riverbank depending on the wind direction. If you follow the West Nodaway River north about a mile, there is a creek that branches off to the east that leads right past where Jacob Butler's farm used to be located. I saw a photograph of the Butler farm taken from the roadside around 1912, that creek area was heavily wooded. The stream then leads to the road where someone could have got into a waiting automobile, or it takes you within a few yards of where Will Piper's farmhouse used to stand. (Courtesy of Google Earth and a 1907 Montgomery County Plot map). I tend to stray away from the car theory because of the proximity of the Butler farmhouse to the road. I'm sure headlights would have been noticed. The creek bed would have provided cover and a convenient path that could be quickly followed in the dark of the night, and it's an important clue also, had they exited the water and walked along the riverbank their scent could have been picked up again and tracked.

Albert Jones (F.F. Jones's son) and Bert McCaul (local garage/pool hall owner) were seen on the morning after the murder (Monday) about 5:00, they were seen driving several miles north of Villisca. The neighbors north of town testified to seeing both of them that morning in court. I think they possibly could have taken Edward and Will Piper to the train station in Grant, after both men changing clothes and shoes at Will's farm, and then the brothers could have traveled up the road a ways and got in McCaul's car. The Pipers possibly boarded or hopped a train heading back south to Clarinda, all in an effort to throw off the bloodhounds. At Clarinda they were spotted by R.H. Thorpe, a salesman from Shenandoah who engaged whom I suspect was Edward in a brief conversation. Thorpe was called to testify at the Wilkerson slander trial in November 1916, where he claimed the morning after the Moore family murders he was on an eastbound train that stopped in Clarinda for 20 minutes for a lunch break. He remained in the smoking car when two men boarded it. One came in the front end and the second man came in the opposite door in the rear of the car. The man who came in the front door walked over to where he was seated and asked for a match, while the stranger appeared to be really nervous, and Thorpe asked if him if he was on drugs. Thorpe described him as 5'10, 150 lbs., with steel grey eyes, cigarette stains on his fingers, sallow complexion and a scar on his Adam's apple area. The other man who was with him stayed at the opposite end of the train car, he was slightly taller with a reddish brown moustache, protruding lip and wore a stiff hat. Thorpe engaged whom he later claimed to be "Blackie" William Mansfield (one of the suspects in the Moore family murders thought to be hired by Frank F. Jones) in a conversation about the Moore murders in Villisca and about whether he thought bloodhounds could track a man. The stranger took out a deck of cards and they played a couple of hands but he was too fidgety to continue. (The playing cards, I think are also a clue; they come up in the Coble and Keller murders). He said both men jumped off before the town of New Market and later that day he witnessed the two men riding on top of a freight car riding back toward Clarinda. (Pg. 2, *The Villisca Review*, November 22nd, 1916) The description of the two men given by Thorpe also matches the Piper Brothers in 1912. Will Piper was 32 years old and had a reddish brown mustache and a protruding lip and Edward was 35, 5'11, black hair and had grey eyes and smoked heavily. According to Patrick Foley, PhD Evolutionary Genetics & Ecology, University of California, Davis, true grey eyes are uncommon and only in 1% of the population. (https://www.quora.com/How-common-are-gray-eyes)

In 1922, R.H. Thorpe made a successful run for Congress as a Republican in Lincoln, Nebraska, ironically the same year that Edward Piper ran for Congress in Corning, Iowa. But in 1936, Thorpe was indicted with three other men in an insurance fraud scheme. He turned state's evidence and was basically caught twisting the truth and throwing his partners under the bus. Thorpe identified at the jail in Red Oak "Insane Blackie" Mansfield as the man on the train the morning of the 10th of June, who did not match his original description given in New Market to the authorities or in court at the trial. I think he very well could have had an encounter with the Piper brothers on that train and changed his story to fit Wilkerson's narrative.

Edward left the area for a few weeks at least. There is an article stating he arrived in Corning from Fresno on the 5th of July and he had been in Oklahoma for a few days checking on some land he owned. (July 6th, 1912, pg. 5, *Adams County Free Press*). This is the only time I read about him owning land in Oklahoma in any of the newspapers; also, I don't think E.B. Piper was in Trigo, his supposed home and the Iowa colony which is five miles from Madera, California. I could not find any sort of record for the Pipers owning a residence in Madera County, however the Pipers did have unclaimed mail at the Madera Post office on June 1st. (*Madera Mercury*, June 1st, 1912). It is possible they roomed at a hotel in Madera. It also seems unlikely that he would go to Iowa and only be there for four days because he left Corning on the 10th, of July to go back to Fresno (Trigo). Bert Simpson, Edward's business partner was seen driving around Villisca the third of June with an "unknown" horse buyer. I would say the term unknown is because the person did not want his name in the paper.

In the June 20th issue of the *Villisca Review*, pg. 6 & 7, there is a list of the Villisca citizens who had contributed to the reward fund for the arrest of the Moore family killer. Curiously enough, Piper & Rose, Col. W.H. Piper, Billie Rose's restaurant or J.W. Roses Horse barn are all not listed as contributing, not even a dollar. Strange, especially as being new members of the community club and just the month before Will Piper was willing to donate $25.00 for the new Armory to be built.

In October, the Commercial Club held a big banquet at the Methodist church in Villisca, and F.F. Jones was the toastmaster; W.H. Piper was in attendance. (*The Villisca Review*, Oct 31st, 1912, pg. 1 and 4).

The Villisca farm fire and the death of Thomas Gill

It seems Will Piper vanished from the newspaper stories from June 10th until the 17th, of July when Will's Villisca farmhouse burned down. It happened in the middle of the night when he was alone. His wife Cora A. was still in Missouri. He had placed a lamp on a tall dresser between the bed and the door; it was his custom to leave a low burning lamp on, which exploded according to reports. (Pg.1, *The Villisca Review*, July 18th, 1912). Will lost all his clothes and his pocket watch, the fire also burned his facial hair. He had to climb out a top floor window and shimmied down and ran across the road to Jacob Butler's farmhouse to call for help and he and Mr. Butler rescued some items and a piano from the home. I thought it strange the article mentions his watch; I wondered if it could have had a broken chain? Like the piece of chain that was found in the downstairs of the Moores' home. Could this fire have been set to cover evidence such as bloody clothes, a possible second murder weapon, or to hide a reddish brown moustache?

Another bit of information I found worth mentioning was that the Moores' home had just been released from quarantine for Scarlet Fever on May, 15th 1912 (Pg. 4 of *The Villisca Review*, May 16th, 1912). The Moores' killer(s) would have had blood contact; he was reported to have possibly eaten there or prepared food. I think it is entirely possible that he or they could have still contracted a virus. In 1912, they did not have proper antibiotics for the treatment of Scarlet Fever; the treatment consisted of just quarantines. The primary source of infection is in the noses and throats of the infected persons and it is spread through coughing or sneezing. It also can be transmitted indirectly by contact with contaminated objects and food. The virus can remain in the blood system of an untreated person for several months. Although rare for an adult to contract the illness, it could be possible. I did struggle with the fact that there had been hundreds of people marching throughout the Moore home the morning after the murders. How come they didn't get Scarlet Fever? So, I looked it up, the virus would have only remained contagious if the blood had been wet or they had been handling contaminated objects. So, did William or even Edward contract Scarlet Fever? Red skin can last up to three weeks, and that would be hard to explain, but getting burned in a fire wouldn't. And if Will had Scarlet Fever at the farm, I'm confident he would not want his sickly wife to contract it. Besides not really wanting that property in the first place, it's a good reason to burn your house and everything in it. Oh, except a piano? As if that not a just bit suspicious itself.

On the tenth of July, E.B. Piper was in the news as going back to Fresno, California with Thomas Gill, a wealthy Corning farmer who had just a year before sold his farmland and started traveling. The fall of 1911, he had just come back from Ireland, and then in May 1912, he went to Canada to view some land he was interested in purchasing. Close to a month after they left in July, on August 4th to be exact, Ed, Ralph Piper, their wives and Thomas were at Zappa Swim Park. Thomas Gill was pushed into the pool by several hoodlums (Pg. 1, Aug 5th, *The San Francisco Call*). The California authorities would question the Pipers; E.B. Piper did not report the incident for 20 minutes and swam to another part of the tank. (Pg. 3, Aug 5th, 1912, *The Los Angeles Times*). The Pipers were suspected of throwing him in but claimed other men did, yet none of them did anything to save or even call for help for Thomas, who they claimed they knew could not swim. (Aug 14th, 1912, pg. 6, *Adams County Free Press*). Edward, of course, played the part of the grief-stricken friend and traveled on the train with Thomas's body back to Camp Grove, Illinois for burial. The obit for Thomas even cast doubt on his fate, though it does state that he drowned, and not that the shock or bruises killed him (*Wyoming Post Herald Illinois*. Aug 14th, 1912). Where did Thomas get the injuries? I also could not find a probate for him in Illinois, so what happened to all of his money? He was a wealthy and unmarried, indeed a prime target, especially since Edward was also a life insurance salesman.

Chapter 4

Show me the Money, Motorcycles, and Scandals

If Senator F.F. Jones paid the Piper Brothers for Moore's murder, where is the money?

To be fair, the Pipers were hard working auctioneers, well at least Will was. But they do seem to have come into a lot of money all at once in 1913. A.P. Simpson and E.B. Piper between the both of them they claimed to have made a total of $75,000 off of land deals in Madera County, California in 1912; I think that is improbable, if not impossible since I could only ever find one land transaction in the *Madera Mercury* under land transactions for both, and both of them would have flooded the *Adams County Free Press* with self-praise articles if that was the truth. (*Madera Mercury*, Nov 2nd, 1912, pg. 1) The 75k is the amount written in Albert P. Simpson's, obviously padded bio in "The History of Fresno County, California" by Paul Vandor (1919, pg. 1456-1457). Simpson was sued by the County of Madera and various individuals over that Trigo property in California. (Foreclosure on lots in Trigo, *Madera Weekly Tribune*, August 21st, 1919).

What are some of the benefits for the Pipers? One thing I noticed is the auction business profits off of Fear. I think political influence for the Pipers must have been intoxicating because everyone wants a Senator and his rich buddies as friends. Senator Frank F. Jones sat on several committees in 1913: Appropriations, Banks, Corporations and Highways. Before the murders, there were several African Americans in Villisca; after the murders, there were none for years that were allowed to live in Villisca. Will Piper had taken legal action over the area south of the track, he wanted it to be cleaned up of vagrants, campers and dumping was soon taken care of by the city. The town street lights that were shut off because of a dispute between the Power Company and City Council were settled the day after the murders. The Armory that Will Piper had wanted and donated money for in May to be built, but the council had to think about it first, was soon built.

I will start with W.H. (Will) Piper

After Will and Cora A. Piper's farmhouse burned down in July, he bought a home on Third Avenue from W.M. Campbell in August for $1,300 and proceeded to remodel it. He had only received 4,500 dollars in insurance money for the property north of town that he paid $300 an acre for in December 1911. He bought the farm from F.F. Jones' neighbor Enarson. The price that was paid for that farm was approximately $9,000, which included his reasonably new home on 4th and his automobile as partial payment. This package deal in 1912 would have been worth a quarter of a million dollars now in 2018. He must have really wanted that location. Anyway, that is the impression I got. In September 1912, Will was selling that 30-acre farm north of Villisca without a house for a discounted price, as in he would make a deal with the first person who seemed interested in it.

In May of 1913, Will traded the Third Avenue home for a 40-acre farm located a mile and one-half east of town, but the Pipers remained in town and moved to a different house on Highland Street. They would move as soon as Mrs. Piper had recovered, as it seemed she had Diphtheria again, and the Third Avenue home was quarantined.

In my opinion, this seems like a whole bunch of shuffling of property, and behind the scenes, Will was buying registered Guernsey dairy cattle. You can flow a significant amount of cash unnoticed through auctions. These are not cheap animals; bulls have been known to sell for over $1,000 in 1912. By June 1914, Will H. Piper was Vice President of the Iowa Guernsey Breeder Association (*Guernsey Breeder's Journal,* Volume 6th, 1914, pg. 44) and was brushing shoulders with some of the most prominent dairy farmers in the United States. That is a huge step up from just learning the dairy business in the fall of 1911. Ask any dairy owner, you cannot just learn the dairy business and in two years, you are suddenly the Vice President of a Breeder's association without a huge influx of cash. Then shortly on August 12th, of 1914, Will was having his own livestock auction of 80 Guernsey plus 25 imported and registered Guernsey cattle. Col. J.E. Mack was the auctioneer (Hoard's Dairyman, Volume 6, pg. 22). This was just part of Piper's herd on his farm, and he continued to raise registered dairy cattle for a few years. Those cattle were worth a big heap of cash, all nicely laundered. I also wondered if he wasn't panicking a bit because Det. James N. Wilkerson showed up in Villisca in April of 1914, asking questions and oddly enough posing as a Texas land agent. Did someone suspect the Pipers … who also were land agents?

Will Piper also purchased a farm in Minnesota in 1914, several newspaper articles about him going to purchase land and visiting his farm there appear in the *Villisca Review* (Aug 20th, 1914, pg. 2. Nov 7th, 1914, pg. 8. and June 9th, 1915, pg. 3).

Edward Piper and family moved back to Corning, Iowa, shortly after Thomas Gill's death in November of 1912. I'm guessing he didn't like the attention he received from the California authorities over Gill's drowning. They started spending money almost immediately, but they had a cover story for the cash which was E.B.'s non-existent land deals. Let's just say Ed's version of how much land he owned and reality had a considerable gap. The lots in Trigo were worth only 10 dollars. (*Madera Mercury*, June 1st, 1917). Trigo, California, had a post office from the fall of 1912 to 1942 and present day Trigo, is an intersection located 7 miles east-southeast of Madera, California.

In January 1913, Ed Piper bought the Bert (A.P.) Simpson residence located on the corner of Eleventh and Adams Street in Corning. In the same month, Ralph and his wife Helga moved back from California, and Ralph was going to help Ed in the sale business. The next few months Ed's and his wife Cora B., made some large land purchases, it seems the Real Estate transfers were in her name. She bought land from J.M. Follis for $4,647, and property from D.F. Sink for $4,750.00 (Feb 5th, 1913, *Adams County Free Press*, pg.2). Then in April Cora bought land from D.S. Driskill for $2,000 (*Adams County Free Press*, April 16th, 1913, pg. 5).

In the spring of 1913, Ed and Ralph opened the Corning Fruit company and started selling cases of different kinds of produce imported from California. In April, Ralph went into business with A.E. Hull selling Indian and Excelsior motorcycles; they were agents, you could see them at the fruit company.

November of 1913, E.B. traded the last piece of California land for an implement business building and the stock in Lenox, Iowa (*Adams County Free Press,* November 12th, 1913, pg. 5). This is an untrue statement because Simpson and Piper were still trying to con people into buying that Trigo land in 1917. He also was elected President of Corning Commercial Club the same year.

I'm going to speculate the payout for the Moore family murders to the Pipers was $20,000, which in 1912 had the same buying power as a half a million dollars in 2018.

Ralph (R.K.) Piper had a love for motorcycles, and in August of 1913, he made national news by taking his Excelsior, the old trusty bike that he had owned for three years and driving it 2,000 miles in 10 days through the Cheyenne reservation in North Dakota which was an impressive feat for anyone in 1913. He also began to race them at the races in Clarinda and Malvern, and in November he won both races. His wife Helga age 23, was a trained dental assistant and was working with Dr. Scanton in Corning. Ralph and Helga announced the birth of their baby boy on April 27th, of 1914; they named him Edward Boyd after his uncle.

Jump ahead to 1915, and this was when Ralph and his brother Edward split paths, whatever happened between the brothers was so severe these men never spoke again.

Ralph (R.K.) now had a Sandy McManus gas engine besides the Indian motorcycle dealership in Corning; I'm guessing he was also selling the merchandise from Edward's implement store he had bought the year before in Lenox, Iowa. In the May, 12th issue of the paper, there was a prominent notice that Ralph Piper was selling everything and leaving Corning. Something apparently had happened to him just to turn his life upside down and to want to leave town suddenly. At the end of the month, the Corning City Council was asking for the resignation of Councilman E.B. Piper on account of serious trouble between him and his brother Ralph's family (Helga) E.B. refused to resign. He claimed he was innocent of the allegations and to resign would show guilt. Will H. Piper spoke on his behalf, but another councilman resigned, saying he was too embarrassed to serve with Mr. Piper. (*Adams County Free Press,* June 9th, 1915, pg. 5). I tried to find proof of what exactly took place at the meeting but the information does not seem to be in the Corning city records. So, I'm speculating that he tried to assault 24-year-old Helga Piper. Ralph and Helga sold everything in Corning and moved to Malvern, Iowa to start over again.

J.W. Noel, Rev J.J. Burris and Mary Peckham

J.W. Noel, a young Villisca photographer, was a surprise witness brought by Wilkerson's defense attorney Mitchell at Wilkerson's slander trial in November and December of 1916. He claimed that one night in May 1916, he and his wife Mae returned home to his studio in Villisca at about 10:30. Noel could hear voices coming from the Jones Warehouse. His house was approximately 14 feet from the warehouse. He peered through the gaps in the wood, and he saw four men talking. He could identify two of the men for sure, one he said was F.F. Jones and another was Albert, his son. He wasn't sure, but he thought the third man was Bert McCaul and the fourth man he did not know. Noel did say he saw the fourth man light a cigar with a cigar lighter, which illuminated the faces of the men. Senator F.F. Jones was heard saying "If I don't win the election I won't have the political pull to put down this thing," and also that Detective Wilkerson needed to be done away with.

Jump ahead to October of 1917, and one evening J.S. Montgomery (Sarah Moore's father) and J.W. Noel were on their way to Nodaway when they noticed lights flashing and a suspicious car by the railroad tracks. They stopped their car and listened for a bit, and they claimed to hear the rattling of chains along the iron rails. After the suspicious vehicle left, the two men went up on the tracks to investigate and found a railroad tie chained to the track with two new log chains. They believed this to be an effort to derail the train that Detective Wilkerson was to be riding on. The two men notified the authorities and bloodhounds were brought to the scene but apparently black pepper had been strewn about and the dogs found nothing.

The log chains were identified by J.T. Latimer of Corning as being purchased at his store. He said the man who made the purchase was about 150 pounds, sandy complexion and about 35 years old. He did think it was strange that he asked for the chains to be wrapped up in paper before he left the store. E.B. Piper had been on the City Council of Corning and was the President of the Corning Commercial Club in 1917. He obviously did not purchase the chains himself, but he could have paid someone to get them for him. The Corning connection is what I'm curious about. And not even 10 days later J.W. Noel would be found dying on the docks of the train depot in Albia, Monroe County with a gunshot to his head. (Albia is 126 miles from Villisca). The coroner of Albia, Hyatt, rule this a suicide, but I have some problems with this theory. Noel was reported to have a typewritten account of his testimony for the Reverend Kelly's trial in his pocket, containing what he was supposed to say. The Reverend Kelly was acquitted of charges in regards to the Moore family and Stillinger girls' murders later in November 1917. I find that a bit too convenient as to imply that his testimony was scripted and rehearsed for him. Noel also mailed a letter to his wife Mae in Villisca from the Creston Station stating he was in the hands of a couple of railroad men and that he felt threatened by them. She would receive this letter shortly before the telephone call with the report her husband had been wounded and taken to the hospital. Noel had thought the harassment from the railroad men was over the investigation about the attempted derailment incident; something is not quite right with all of this narrative. He had financial problems, but I don't think it was enough to cause him to be suicidal. Why kill yourself over a hundred miles away in Albia? And why make up this story about the railroad men? After Noel's death, J.S. Montgomery immediately changed his story about what happened the night that both of them found the wooden tie chained to the tracks.

One of the witnesses stood out to me in the Grand Jury inquest in March 1917, and it is a shame he was not checked out better by investigators because he was one of the key figures in my determination on Frank F. Jones as being responsible for hiring the murder of the Moore family. Reverend J.J. Burris, who at the time claimed to be living in Oklahoma, had started corresponding with Senator F.F. Jones in 1916, after reading about the investigation and slander trial of Bert Wilkerson. The Senator claimed he had turned over these letters to the County Attorney, Wenstrand, before the Wilkerson slander trial the year before and only now did the Grand Jury call the Reverend Burris to testify. He said that in 1913, he had been a pastor at the Church of Christ at Radersburg, Montana. One day he was called to the hotel bed of a dying young man by friends, who said the man wanted to confess his sins. The man said he suffered from heavy drinking and he had murdered eight people in Villisca, Iowa, but to please keep his confession secret as not to hurt his family members, and then he died. Reverend Burris wrote the man's name down but lost it. He did remember the man was 25 to 30 years old and had been a blacksmith by trade in Villisca. Reverend Burris also stated he had once lived in Iowa and preached in Adams County but only knew Senator F.F. Jones by their correspondence. (pg. 1 of *The Villisca Review*, March 17th, 1917).

The good ole Reverend Burris turns out to be Reverend liar, liar, pants on fire! A few days later after people started to look into this story, the blacksmith that is referred to in Burris' story, Zerrel Morrow, had a sister, Izola Morrow, and she was not happy about having her brother's name tarnished by being connected to this horrific crime. Apparently, there were witnesses at Zerrel's deathbed and **No** preachers were present. (March 21st, pg. 1, *The Villisca Review*. Reverend John Burris was a 52 year old Carbon Town, Iowa, Methodist minister who did live in Montana at the time of Zerrel's death, but Burris also had deep family ties to Monroe and Adams counties. In September 1915, John's son William Burris was severely injured in a mining accident at the Buxton No. 17 Mine in Monroe County. (*The Albia Republican*, September 9th, 1915, pg. 1). He was riding on top of a railcar when they collided into each other smashing him against walls of the mine. He was taken to the miner's hospital where he later died and was then buried in Corning, Adams County. Why would this minister lie to a Grand Jury for Senator F.F. Jones? Could his son's life insurance accident payoff be tied to helping the Senator off of a murder charge? Edward had a connection to the railroad through C&NW Division Superintendent N.C. Allen. (The C&NW railroad owned the Buxton No 17 mine). In 1914, Edward was lobbying him for a new train depot in Corning (*Adams County Free Press,* January, 28th, 1914, pg. 1), putting to good use those knowing a Senator "perks". Senator Frank F. Jones also served on the Appropriations Committee with Senator Frederic Larrabee, Chair of the Railroad Committee. The Highway Committee that Senator Jones served on, Senator John T. Clarson from Albia was also a member and he was the Chair of the Mines and Mining Committee. It seems to me a lot of these stories have connections to the railroad and in these two counties Adams and Monroe, both of which the Piper family also had deep ties. Is this all a coincidence? I don't think so; I think it's a clue.

The Peckham home is located approximately 30 feet from the Moore family home; Johnny Hauser now lives in Mary Peckham's home. I watched an interview with him where he talked about that he has been home in bed with a TV on and has heard screams coming from the Moore home, when people got little freaked out in the middle of the night during a paranormal investigation. Mary lived with her husband Orlando who was the city grave digger and her son Ernest who still lived with them. Mary Peckham testified at the Coroner's inquest she heard or saw nothing the night of the murders. The murders of the Moore family and the Stillinger girls pushed Mary Peckham over the edge and really she should be considered the ninth victim of this tragedy. By December her mental health had deteriorated from a nervous breakdown, and her daughter who was married to Dr. Edgar Clayton Hough came back to Villisca and took her back to Bozeman, Montana. Dr. Hough had a practice and ranch located near Bozeman. Strange thing is they did not take her to their home at the ranch but to a hotel where they had to carry her in and, poor elderly Mary Peckham died in that hotel a few days later and was sent back to Villisca for the burial. (*The Daily Missoulian,* Missoula, Montana, Dec 14th, 1912, pg. 6). It was claimed it was from the shock of discovering the murders; only thing is she testified at the Coroner's inquest she stayed on the porch and did not go in, but I think after she had time to process what had happened she possibly did see something the night of the murders. Why usher her off to Montana? If Harriet had great concern for her mother then why take her to a strange hotel to die and not the ranch, or she could have left her in Villisca at the house she had shared with her family for 20 years; the daughter's actions seem a bit callus to me. The Houghs were very wealthy and often had visitors staying at their ranch, were they afraid of what she would say in her state of mind at their home or in her own home in Villisca?

The Houghs lived on Fourth Street, a few houses away from the Pipers when both couples lived in Villisca. Mary's daughter Harriet was a personal friend of Will Piper's wife Cora (Ora), perhaps Ora's only friend, and as both ladies never were able to have children, they shared a common bond. Harriet's husband Edgar was also one of Ora's doctors and she was often sick and could not leave her home. Colonel Will Piper handled several livestock sales for Dr. Hough in Montana. Will Piper also handled the sale of the ranch for Harriet after her husband suddenly died at Harrison, Montana, in March of 1918. (*The Butte Miner,* March 31st, 1918, pg. 2).

The Houghs also come up in connection to the Reverend Burris' false story about the confession of Zerrel Morrow which also took place in Montana. Zerrel's sister Izola was staying at the Hough's ranch at the time of her brother's death in 1913, and that is why she knew and could prove that Reverend Burris' story was false.

I suppose one could wonder if the Reverend J.J. Burris was actually at Mary Peckham's hotel death bedside and not Zerrel Morrow's. Possibly, Burris was bribed by Frank Jones, with whom he had been corresponding through letters, to change his story and the blacksmith that had been spoken about as the person who murdered the Moore family, was actually Mary Peckham pointing the blame on Will Piper the current husband of Ora Paulin Piper, the widow of John Paulin one of Villisca's blacksmiths who had passed away in 1906.

What about Ralph Piper, Malvern Manor and the fate of the Evil Piper Brothers?

Ralph, Helga and their son little Edward moved to Malvern in 1915, after the fallout with his brother Edward. Ralph bought the Empress Theater from Joe Mahoney in June 1915. In 1917, he went into business with H.H. Lathen selling Studebaker automobiles by September of that year; Ralph was the sole owner of the car dealership and mechanics garage. In 1940, Ralph bought the Cottage Hotel from Cuba Cox, a single mother who ran a restaurant and rented rooms in the decaying old hotel. Ralph kept her on as the manager, and the two of them began to fix the old hotel up. He was the one who lined the walls in the front lobby with knotty pine, which you can still see inside the Manor. The first floor was little apartments and the second floor of the hotel was newly remodeled rooms with new plumbing fixtures. He also installed a big neon sign that said Piper Hotel out front. He was very proud of that sign. Ralph and Helga hadn't lived together for a long time, and I'm not sure when the two moved to separate houses, but in 1941 after their son Edward joined the Army, h sold his businesses in Malvern and closed up his home and moved into the Piper Hotel with his beloved Cuba.

I think Ralph and Cuba had been romantically involved since after her divorce in 1931. They often took trips together, they were in love, and I don't think they cared one bit how the people of Malvern gossiped. Ralph was a City Councilman for years and by all accounts liked by the whole community. Ralph died in 1949. He had an altercation with two of his employees over an overturned jeep and he dropped dead of a heart attack outside of Malvern. He left the hotel to Cuba in his will and then poor Cuba would spend six years fighting her then ex-son-in-law Eddie Piper in court for her and Ralph's pet parrot Pat. Ralph's son Eddie and Cuba's daughter Peggy had been married and divorced. Cuba Cox sold The Piper hotel in 1956, and it was made into a rest home, Nishna cottage.

I don't think Ralph was trying to intimidate Johnny Hauser that night of their encounter. I think he just wanted to tell someone his story and he felt Johnny was someone to whom he could relate. The night of our investigation at the manor when my daughter awoke to sounds of old music, I could almost picture Ralph and Cuba up late having a drink and dancing. They spent some of their happiest times there. Maybe that's the reason for his reaching across the veil to tell his story.

Edward and Will Piper were Dr. Jekyll and Mr. Hyde type of bad men, only with money and influence. When things heated up in Villisca with the accusations against Senator F.F. Jones flying left and right and the multiple Grand Jury sessions, the Pipers, especially Will, traveled to their ranch in Murdo and Oakton, Jones County, South Dakota. Both are small towns in what's called "The Gateway" to the Black Hills. In 1910, the population of Murdo was 372 (it was like their "Hole in the Wall" hideout). They had an auction business and owned the Northwestern Land Agency in Murdo. Strange thing is I could only ever find newspaper advertisements for a few of these sales after checking through old South Dakota newspapers at the digital archives at the Library of Congress. Nothing like they were proclaiming in Villisca and Corning, Iowa newspapers. In fact, for some of the customers that they said they had been doing business for, I could not find any kind of a record. The Piper brothers were known for printing their own sale bills, so this is all fictitious and I do not have an answer for why they would do this other than they were possibly hiding something or money.

Edward was on the City Council in Corning 1913-1915 and was the President of the Corning Commercial Club from 1915-1919, so it come as no surprise that in 1916, the film "The Birth Of a Nation" played in Corning and was a big hit, replaying several times the next year. (March 4th, 1916, pg. 5, *Adams County Free Press*). "The Birth of a Nation" is the Silent epic drama film that was directed by D.W. Griffith, having been adapted from the book "The Clansmen," written by Thomas Dixon, Jr. Most people attribute this film to the reawakening of the Ku Klux Klan in America. In 1916, a newspaper clipping warning from the Ku Klux Klan threatening anyone who told on another Clansman appeared; I'm not sure if this was "For Real" or part of the hype of the film, ironically it appears directly under an article about the Jones-Wilkerson slander suit cost to the County in Red Oak (December 23rd, 1916 pg. 9, *Adams County Free Press*).

Will and Edward Piper started to buy land in Louisiana in 1916 and 1920 but this seems also a secret endeavor from both of them. In 1917, Will's wife Cora A. went to Lake Charles, Louisiana. (October 10th, 1917, pg. 8, *The Villisca review*) (November 14th, 1917, pg. 10, *The Villisca Review*). A newspaper article appeared in the May 15th, 1920 edition of the *Adams County Free Press*, pg. 1, about Edward Piper was looking for timber land in a swamp by Baton Rouge, Louisiana and Ed had an encounter with a mean alligator. The men that were with Edward said it was a good thing the alligator decided to leave, not serious but all in jest and Ed bought that swamp with the mean alligator. As much as Edward Piper seems to be a "good guy", he is not. Between May 1918, and October of 1919, there were a series of famous axe murders in New Orleans that seemed similar in ways to the axe murders of 1911-1912. Only the New Orleans murders seemed to target Italian immigrant grocery store owners. I don't think I have to remind anyone about how racist the Ku Klux Klan is, and was.

There is a famous letter that is attributed to the Axe man of New Orleans;

Hell, March 13, 1919
Esteemed Mortal of New Orleans:

They have never caught me and they never will. They have never seen me, for I am invisible, even as the ether that surrounds your earth. I am not a human being, but a spirit and a demon from the hottest hell. I am what you Orleanians and your foolish police call the Axeman.

When I see fit, I shall come and claim other victims. I alone know whom they shall be. I shall leave no clue except my bloody axe, besmeared with blood and brains of he whom I have sent below to keep me company.

If you wish you may tell the police to be careful not to rile me. Of course, I am a reasonable spirit. I take no offense at the way they have conducted their investigations in the past. In fact, they have been so utterly stupid as to not only amuse me, but His Satanic Majesty, Francis Josef, etc. But tell them to beware. Let them not try to discover what I am, for it were better that they were never born than to incur the wrath of the Axeman. I don't think there is any need of such a warning, for I feel sure the police will always dodge me, as they have in the past. They are wise and know how to keep away from all harm.

Undoubtedly, you Orleanians think of me as a most horrible murderer, which I am, but I could be much worse if I wanted to. If I wished, I could pay a visit to your city every night. At will I could slay thousands of your best citizens (and the worst), for I am in close relationship with the Angel of Death.

Now, to be exact, at 12:15 (earthly time) on next Tuesday night, I am going to pass over New Orleans. In my infinite mercy, I am going to make a little proposition to you people. Here it is:

I am very fond of jazz music, and I swear by all the devils in the nether regions that every person shall be spared in whose home a jazz band is in full swing at the time I have just mentioned. If everyone has a jazz band going, well, then, so much the better for you people. One thing is certain and that is that some of your people who do not jazz it out on that specific Tuesday night (if there be any) will get the axe.

Well, as I am cold and crave the warmth of my native Tartarus, and it is about time I leave your earthly home, I will cease my discourse. Hoping that thou wilt publish this, that it may go well with thee, I have been, am and will be the worst spirit that ever existed either in fact or realm of fancy

--The Axeman,

When I read it, I have to say it reads like a mixture of the serial killer H.H. Holmes' ghoulish quote with a dash of smartass, all meant to terrorize a community. Edward wrote some rather strange letters to newspapers also, several I have listed in my notes. A couple of things about this letter caught my attention, the use of the word Invisible, the KKK called themselves the Invisible empire and the constant use of I AM, Edward seemed to use I AM all the time in his advertisements and letters to the newspapers. From what I can tell Edward was supposed to be in Oakton, South Dakota, during some of those murders but there is no way of telling if he did not just drop his wife Cora B. at their ranch and leave again like he did in Trigo, California in 1911-1912. So, the jury is out on that one and maybe this story will inspire a researcher to find out exactly what the brothers were doing and where the Pipers owned land in Louisiana.

Edward Piper ran as an Independent for Congress and later switched to Democrat in 1922. He lost the race to J.P. Daughton which should not be a surprise, because Edward and Cora Piper were wanted by the County Court in California over multiple land fraud claims. (*Madera Tribune*, October 22, 1921, pg. 4, Alias summons). In 1934, the Pipers sold everything in Corning and moved to the Piper farm in Alabama to be closer to his son Carl Piper's family. Not sure when he bought this farm but it was before 1922, there is an article about Carl working on the Piper farm in Alabama and having to take care of 13 Negro families, sounds more like a Plantation. (*Adams County Free Press,* November 16th, 1921, pg. 5).

Edward Piper also traveled regularly to Mobile, Alabama from Corning, Iowa to the family ranch which takes you through Birmingham, Alabama, and coincidently between 1919 and 1924 immigrant shopkeepers and interracial couples were the target of a mob gang or a solo axe murderer that left 18 people dead and 16 injured.

Edward and his wife Cora spent years traveling back and forth between Corning, Iowa and the ranch, it seems he couldn't stay away from his "comfort zone" and he would always returns to Corning, except for his last train ride. Edward Boyd Piper died August 20th, 1958, aged 80 and Cora Bell Piper died April 24th, 1973, aged 92. Both are buried in Mobile, Alabama.

Will H. Piper (Col. W.H.) died in Branch, Arkansas, March 14th, 1958 and Cora (Ora) May 24th, 1940. Both are buried at Villisca. I could not help but feel sorry for Will, only Ralph's family showed up to his funeral. (March 20th, 1958, *The Villisca Review*, pg.1). In Cora's obit, it claims she was a Presbyterian from Corning, but that is not the case. The Spencers were Methodist and Ora continued to be a Methodist. This mistake seems odd unless her husband Will gave them the information wrong on purpose. Maybe because tensions still existed between churches in Villisca, or it was a simple misprint. (May 30th, 1940, *Villisca Review*, pg. 5).

Chapter 5

1910, 1911 to June 10, 1912 Notes

This section is two and half years of what I feel is relevant information pertaining to the Pipers and the townsfolk of Villisca leading up to the murders in Villisca. Most are from newspaper articles and my notes. A bit tedious, but I feel if I'm going to accuse a person of murder even if after 100 years, I probably better show the information that led me to this conclusion.

1910

January - Tuesday the 11th, The Piper brothers have a sale in Villisca. The clerks for the sale are (Albert) Davies and (Albert) Jones. They also have the E.M. Moore auction on the 25th, and Mayor F.L. Ingman is the Clerk (*The Villisca Review*, Jan 20th, 1910)/

February - E.B. cries a sale at Hopkins, Missouri. (*Adams County Free Press*, February 26th, 1910, pg. 9). The Corning mayor appoints E.B. to the good roads convention in Des Moines on March 8th and 9th (*Burlington Hawk Eye*, February 13th, 1910, pg. 8).

March - W.H. manages and cries a successful horse and pony sale with the popular Iowa horse auctioneer Colonel John T. Graham. The horse sale is a big event in Villisca and draws people from all over Iowa. (pg. 1 of *The Villisca Review,* March 17th, 1910). - Later that month, W.H. Piper withdraws his name along with T.M. Scott for Candidate for Villisca City Councilman (Pg. 1 of *The Villisca Review,* March 24th, 1910).

April - E.B. and his son Carl return from a two-week stay in Mexico visiting Matt Gourd (*Adams County Free Press,* April 2nd, 1910, pg. 7). Matt Gourd is a fellow Corning man whom E.B. went to Mexico with in '09 and purchased 700 acres and Matt 260 in Tampico (*Adams County Free Press,* March 24th, 1909, pg. 5).

May - E.B. goes to Mexico with parties from Greenfield, Adair County, Bloomfield, and Davis County, Iowa to view the land he is selling as a land agent for Mexico. Davis County happens to be the heart of the old "Hairy Nation."

July - E.B. and A.P. Simpson from Mt. Etna, Iowa are now land agents for California Co-Operative Land Company, they have an office, Farmers Nation Bank, in Corning and are offering land near Fresno for $40 dollars an acre and trips to view the property, no money down at purchase. (*Adams County Free Press,* July 23rd, 1910, pg. 12).

August - (*Adams County Free Press,* August 17th, 1910, pg. 3)/ Col. E.B. Piper left yesterday with 15 land-seekers to Mexico.

September - (*Adams County Free Press*, September 3rd, 1910, pg. 9). E.B. Piper and party return from Mexico, where he visited Matt Gourd.

November - E.B.'s family and the Simpson family go to Fresno California (*Adams County Free Press*, November 5th, 1910, pg. 9).

December - The 5th , 8th and 10th of the month the Piper brothers have sales in Villisca. Two of them are at J.W. Rose's (Billie) horse barn, located two blocks east of the Villisca national bank, where F.F. Jones and F.L. Ingham are the clerks.(*The Villisca Review*, December 1st, 1910). Edward is supposed to be at these sales.

1911

January - Close-out Sale- auction on January, 19th, the Piper Brothers, and Albert Jones is the Clerk (pg. 11 of *The Villisca Review,* January 12th, 1911). The Piper Brothers have three sales on the 24th, 25th, and the 27th the clerks are Frank Heaton F.F. Jones and F.L. Ingman (pg. 9 of The Villisca Review, January 19th, 1911). On January 30th, J.W. Hiatt, who rents and lives on E.B.'s Piper's farm north of Villisca, has a severe accident and is run over by his wagon (he dies within days). (pg. 5 of *The Villisca Review*, February 2nd , 1911).

February - The Piper Brothers. - They have three sales listed for the 14th, 17th and 18th; F.L. Ingman, and F.F. Jones are the clerks. (pg. 10 of *The Villisca Review,* Feb 9th, 1911).

The same newspaper has an article for Billie Rose and W.H. Piper's second annual horse auction, a big event for Villisca, and it is advertised throughout the state. (pg. 12, *The Villisca Review*, February 9th, 1911). The Piper Brothers have four sales for the 21st, 22nd, 23rd, and 24th of February in the Villisca area. Clerks are F.F. Jones and, F.L. Ingman and Elmer Brown (pg. 9 of *The Villisca Review*, February 16th, 1911).

March - Big Horse Sale at Villisca. W.H. Piper and J.W. Rose (Billie Rose). The horse auction on the 9th and 10th, this is supposed to be the biggest in southwestern Iowa, and over 400 head are consigned. Orville A. Jones (who runs an Auctioneers school in Chicago) and John T. Graham from Des Moines are co-auctioneers, and the clerks are F.L. Ingman and F.F. Jones. (pg. 1 of *The Villisca Review*, March 2nd, 1911) - The longtime Villisca Mayor E.C. Gibb resigns (pg. 8 of *The Villisca Review*, March 9th, 1911). - Last Saturday (on the 11th) E.B. and family along the J.H. Old, Chas Shupa and The Thompsons started for Fresno, California. Mr. Piper will engage in the land business. (*Adams County Free Press*, March 18th, 1911, pg. 7).

April - Letter from Ed Piper, he writes a lengthy letter from Fresno back to Corning that reads like an award acceptance speech (*Adams County Free Press*, April 5th, pg. 8).

May - Julia A. Hiatt, the widow of the late J.W. Hiatt who had lived on the Ed Piper property northeast of Villisca, brings suit against E.B. Piper in court for auctioning off of the

Hiatt's personal property along with the property from Piper /Hiatt sheep farm and keeping the proceeds. The First National Bank brings suit also for the money they had loaned this partnership (Adams County Free Press, May 10th, pg. 10). -Col. Piper. Here, Col. E.B. Piper arrived in Corning from Fresno, California; on train No. 6, Monday of this week. (*Adams County Free Press*, May 17th, 1911, pg. 5). -E.P. Crandall purchases a 1911 Brush Runabout auto from Jones Store. W.H. Piper goes with Jones's Store manager J.L. Palmquist to Omaha to pick it up. (pg. 5 of *The Villisca Review*, May 25th , 1911).

June - W.H. Piper advertisement for trips to Chelsea, South Dakota and return. Piper is the land agent (pg. 7 of *The Villisca Review*, June 1st, 1911).

August - Piper Bros. Advertisement states E.B. will back on September 1 (pg. 6 of *The Villisca Review*, August 10th, 1911).

September - Grand Public Sale, September 5th, 1911. A.P. Simpson is selling out his Mt. Etna Farm that had belonged to his wife's father, Silas Morton, after whom the village of Morton Mills, Iowa is named. Also, F.F. Jones has a bank branch in Morton Mills. The Piper Brothers are the auctioneers, but not sure if E.B. is in Iowa (*Adams County Free Press*, September 2nd, 1911, pg. 5). Col. E.B. Piper returned (to Iowa) from California, Wednesday(27th), and will remain here and look after his sale and other business. *(Adams County Free*

Press, September 29th, 1911, pg. 4)-Horse Sale -Piper Rose (Villisca Horse Sale Company) at J.W. Rose's Barn Saturday, Sept 30th Piper & Mainquist are the auctioneers, F.L. Ingman, Clerk (pg. 3 of *The Villisca Review,* Sept 28th, 1911). The same page, Closing-out Sale- October 5th, auction and the Auctioneers are Piper Bros. -E.B. Piper will be at this sale. F.E. Shane is the clerk.

October - Ed Piper was in Red Oak the latter part of last week looking after business matters. (*Adams County Free Press,* October 11th, 1911, pg. 10). -E.B. Piper of Corning spent last Friday (6th) at Villisca with his brother Col. W.H. Piper (pg. 3 of *The Villisca Review,* October 12th, 1911)--Why Not Have a Horse Show?- Meeting of Businessmen and Citizens is called for Friday evening of this week to discuss the proposition. Mayor F.L. Ingman W.H. Piper and Biller Rose want to have annual Horse shows in Villisca (pg. 2 of *The Villisca Review,* October 19th, 1911). (A.P. Simpson, E.B.'s California Land Co-partner) has an advertisement which offers a trip to Trigo, California leaving on the 14th of October, 1911, it has stops at Villisca and Red Oak (Adams County Free Press, October 7th, 1911, pg. 6). W.H. and E.B. Piper have an auction south of Villisca on the 18th of Oct F.L. Ingman is the clerk (pg. 9 of *The Villisca Review,* October 12th, 1911). Court in Session, the First Nation Bank's case against E.B. Piper is to take place on the 19th of October (*Adams County*

Free Press, October 18th, 1911). Two advertisements stand out on this day, one for Piper Rose Horse sales in Villisca, W.H. Piper and Mainquist are the auctioneers, and another 4 X larger one for E.B. Piper, stating he is Iowa's Greatest Farm Auctioneer (*Adams County Free Press,* October 21st, 1911, pg. 10). – I Will Stay. E.B. has an advertisement declaring he will stay and work with his brother, also he is still selling California land (*Adams County Free Press,* October 25th, 1911). W.H. Piper is the auctioneer for a Fairview Guernsey Sale; the article states he is new to the dairy cattle business (pg. 1 of The Villisca Review, October 26th, 1911).

November - E.B. places a large obscure advertisement in the *Adams County Free Press,* it reads: You can't keep a good man down, did you know that? I have lost some of my sales this fall, of course. Do you know why? I will tell you! I was gone and people did not know where I was, I did not know myself whether I could come sell sales. I have at least twenty letters from people who have held sale who wanted me to cry their sales. Did you know that? No, of course, you didn't don't think for a moment that I am dead. Not on your life. I am here. Now I will whisper something in your ear, and listen and see if I have lied. I have dated forty sales, besides all other business I have done since I came home I dated five sales alone at Frank McGregor's sale and, I dated six sales in the office Saturday. Now if you fellows think I am a liar, watch my sale bills and watch my sale and prices. Anybody can say sold, but don't forget the PRICE: and don't forget I have made the price for years - E.B. Piper Livestock Auctioneer. (*Adams County Free Press,* November 8th, 1911 pg. 4)

Saw the Sell Horses - Article from the editor of the *Corning Free Press* talking about the big horse sale in Villisca . How they were started by W.H. Piper three years ago and now he's in partnership with Billie Rose. He also commented on the crappy electric street light service. (pg. 2 of *The Villisca Review,* November 16th, 1911).

December - Buys Small Farm-W.H. Buys the Louis Enarson 30 acre farm, north of Villisca (about 1 mile close to the West Norway River) for the enormous amount of $300 dollars an acre. His new home on West Fourth Street and his automobile were taken as part of the payment. (pg. 5 of *The Villisca Review,* December 14th, 1911). - E.B. returned to California the fore part of last week. He will look after his land interests near Fresno for a few weeks and expects to return to Corning about the first of February to look after some sale which demands his attention. (*Adams County Free Press,* December 27th, 1911 pg. 5).

1912

January - Successful Sale W.H. Piper is the auctioneer for a big Guernsey cattle sale in Iowa City. He is even asked to go to Virginia to cry a sale there; some of the cows sold for $167 or as much as the average acre of land in 1912. (pg. 1 of *The Villisca Review*, January 4th, 1912).

February - Horse Sale February 7- Piper &Rose Horse Sale, E.B. and W.H. are the auctioneers. Not sure if E.B. shows up? (*The Villisca Review*, February 1st , 1912, pg. 1).

March - Full page ad for these monthly horse sales at Billie Rose's sale barn F.L. Ingman and P.D. Minick are the clerks (*The Villisca Review*, March 14th, 1912, pg. 4).

April - W.H. Piper's wife Cora A. goes to Excelsior, Missouri for a month's stay, and she remains there all summer (*The Villisca Review*, April 25th, 1912, pg. 8).

May - W.H. Piper offers to donate $25 for the new armory to be built; the Council decided it needed to discuss it first. (*The Villisca Review*, May 2nd , 1912 pg. 2).

 - Addition Club Members - Piper & Rose are new members to the Commercial Club (*The Villisca Review*, May 2nd, pg. 8).

June - Horse sale at Billie's Rose's on June 8th, 1912.This is two days before the Moore family murders. W.H. Piper, auctioneer and F.L. Ingman, clerk.

1914

The Sycamore Grove members of W.O.W. (Woodmen of the World) held their meeting at E.B. Piper's home in Corning (*Adams County Free Press*, October 10, 1914, Saturday, Page 4).

Chapter 6

Is Colonel E.B. Piper the Infamous Midwest Axe Murderer?

E.B. Piper very well could be the Midwest axe murder. But how I can prove it? I can't. It has been over 100 years since these horrific crimes and unless there is DNA evidence from any of these crimes preserved somewhere, I think it will always remain a mystery. What I can show you are reasons that I'm convinced he is the Axeman and why he would be in certain cities on certain dates and that he was traveling the trains at the time of the murders.

Edward was a member of Woodmen of the World, a salesman for New York Life insurance company and a land agent, besides his many other occupations. Traveling salesmen go to big events and fairs, where they make new contacts; also, most of the bigger cities had a regional insurance office where he could have been provided with client information, relocations and possible new clients. Moreover, a person could purchase client lists from other salesmen. Some of the axe murders victims had just re-located or had recent lifestyle changes that would require a change to an insurance policy. I think he picked and chose his victims from information provided

67

through the insurance companies. We can't overlook the fact that several of the victims had Woodmen connections.

I think that Edward Piper committed all of the murders alone, with the exception of the Paola, Kansas and Villisca, Iowa murders, which were business. The other axe murders had something about their name or address that related to the Piper family, and these were for his sick twisted pleasure.

In 1902, Edward sued in court in Adams County, Iowa, his mother Grace, his brothers Will Harrison (W.H.), Albert Chase (A.C.), Ralph Knox (R.K.) and his sister Ida May for land left to them in their father Lon K.'s estate. Not sure if Edward was cut out of his father's estate and wanted his fair share, but on October 15th, 1902, he won. The date October 15th is also the date of the W.H. Showman family murders in Ellsworth, Kansas nine years later.

According to Dr. Elizabeth Yardley, Director of the Center for Applied Criminology at Birmingham City University, U.K. there are five essential characteristics of a serial killers

1. A Power junkie

2. A Manipulator

3. An Egotistical Bragger

4. A Superficial Charmer

5. An Average Joe

When I read this, it was like they knew Colonel E.B. Piper

Serial Killers have what is called a Modus Operandi (M.O.) which in the Axe murders is the sneaking in and bludgeoning his victims in bed. They also have a signature (the crime scenes) and pattern (names). A killer will change or refine his MO to fit the circumstances. I'm no expert but from what I have read in books and online, Edward as an offender showed a mix of organized and disorganized behavior in his murders. I think exploding in a fit of rage and bashing people's heads in is a type of stress relief and an aphrodisiac for Ed Piper. It might be possible he had a drug addiction to cocaine. Monroe County had mines and railroads, both of which were known for "drug" hotspots.

Edward Piper was also a very intelligent con-artist. He claimed he was buying and selling property all over the country but basically he and his partner Albert Simpson were swindling people out of their money and property. By 1922 the County of Madera, California was looking for both Edward and his wife Cora or their aliases. Apparently, the Pipers were selling land they did not own. A.P. Simpson and his wife also had several legal actions brought against them by the state of California between the years of 1917-1925.

In "The Illustrated History of Monroe County, Iowa," by Frank Hickenlooper, 1896, Chapter 18 is about some battles with the "Hairy Nation". These folks settled their differences and even for recreation would fight and beat the crap out of other clans with clubs. Edward was a teacher/Principal in Monroe County, he would have read or perhaps taught from this book. Not to mention the Piper family has several mentions in the book.

The use of a blunt instrument for the crime: every household in those days had an axe around the home for daily chores, it is what called a "weapon of opportunity". Also, Ed was a hog farmer at times, and that is exactly how they killed a hog for the butcher, with the blunt side of an axe to the skull.

In his twisted mind, he was using Nat Turner's tactics of sneaking inside and attacking people as they slept, which were stories he would have been told as a child from his grandparents who lived through the Nat Turner rebellion in Virginia, August 22nd, 1831. Nat Turner felt religious justification for the murders and in several of the letters that were written to authorities about the axe murders, the purported killer seems to have the same religious tone about him and Edward loved to be in the newspapers and write letters to them. It would be something if those letters still existed because a handwriting expert could compare Edward's signature.

I noticed a connection between when the Midwest axe murders started in 1911, and when Edward and Will go their own ways for a bit. This is when Edward started traveling all over the Midwest region, Mexico and to California/West Coast all by railway and his brother Will entered into business relationships with others. Some of the murders happened within days or even coincided with the big horse sales his brother W.H. was having in Villisca at Billie Rose's or the court appearances that Edward had to make in Red Oak. A lot of the male axe victims were named William or even had the initials W.H. like his brother's name. I think Edward was jealous of his brother's success in Villisca and bottled up his rage, which exploded in the axe murder violence. When Edward lived and worked in Iowa, he was a big fish in a small pond, he was secure in his element and making money as an auctioneer. People treated Ed as a celebrity, he was in the newspapers daily. He left home, leaving that security and power, where he was just another sales person on the train. He also would have had a lot of stress keeping up his many lies and business deals.

From the letters and newspaper advertisements he took out in 1910-1912, he seems a bit unhinged, to me anyway. If you have to take out a full-page ad in the hometown newspapers to declare you are not a liar. You are probably a liar.

Women, I suspect Edward was a sexual predator. He seems to have had a problem as a school teacher, and he had a problem with his brother Ralph's wife. Also, I suspect he might have had something to do with Cecil Dodd's death, in 1909. Cecil Dodd, age 20, a stenographer who lived in Red Oak would be found dead on the railroad tracks by Malvern, Iowa; it was believed she threw herself out the train window or was hurled. Her head and face were mutilated (*The San Bernardino County Sun*, December 30th, 1909, pg. 5) & (Quad City Times, December 29th, 1909). Ed's sister, Ida May Piper, married Luke Dodd on June 24th, 1908, at her mother's home in Albia (*Adams County Free Press*, July 1st, 1908). I could not determine if they were related. The last name Dodd, being young and pretty might have been all it took to become one of his victims.

He often left his wife Cora B. and his son Carl for months at a time in Trigo, California; she had his brother Ralph and Helga for support. By his admission in 1913, Edward said he had been traveling for the last three years. He would often visit schools which I suppose is not out of the ordinary; he was a school Principal at Mt. Edna, Iowa. (*Madera Mercury* #39 13th, January 1912). When the Pipers did move back to Corning, Iowa, his wife Cora B. would host parties for young girls at their home. I could see it if they had a girl of their own, but Carl, their son, was about 14 years old at the time. I find this creepy.

At the Moore's house and several other murders, anyway, the ones that I think are related, the windows, mirrors and faces/bodies of the dead were covered; the killer would linger in the house for a while after the murders, and even washed up in a basin. Mirrors and windows were covered or the shades were drawn. The Pipers originally come from Washington County, Virginia, it is part of the Southern Appalachian Mountains, and there are death customs specific to this region. They would lay the deceased out on a cooling board to wash the body, also they would soak rags in soda water, aspirins or camphor and cover the face to preserve it for the wake, to keep the skin from discoloring. In some cases the body was covered completely with a sheet and bound to the board to prevent the corpse from sitting up on its own. Family and friends would sit with the dead all night, singing, eating food and waiting for the spirit to leave the body. ("Burial Practices in Southern Appalachia," by Donna W. Stansberry School of graduate studies at East Tennessee University). Every mirror in the home would be draped with dark cloth, and the hands of the clock would be stopped (*Sitting up with the Dead: Lost Appalachian Burial Customs*). Why cover the face of someone that you have destroyed? I've thought about this quite a bit. Although not precisely the same, it might be a case of this is what he had seen done as a child, with the passing of the original Mountain folk in Monroe County. After the initial rage was over, I think it disgusted him and perhaps in his own way he was showing remorse for what had occurred.

The Casaway Family

Let me start with the Alfred Louis Castaway family (notice the initials A.C.); this murder happened on the 22nd, of March 1911 in San Antonio, Texas. Alfred, a black man, was a school janitor for many years at Grant, and by all accounts he was well liked. He was also married to a white woman, which was taboo in those days. The bodies of the Alfred, age 52, his wife Elizabeth, age 37, and their three little children Jose, age 6, Louise, age 3 and little baby Alfred, 5 months, all were found dead, killed with the blunt side of an axe. Alfred had a cloth over what was left of his head. So, could E.B. have murdered these folks? Edward was supposed to go with his family and other Corning residents to Fresno on March 11th (*Adams County Free Press*, March 18th, 1911, pg. 7). There is no way of telling if he didn't send his wife and Carl on to Kansas City with the other Corning, Iowa folks making the trip. This is something Edward often did. He would ride part way with his wife and then take another train to continue with his business; also, his brother Ralph and wife had been living in the Fresno area already. Edward had been making regular trips down to Tampico, Mexico in 1910, to see Matt Gourd and check the land he had purchased about every three months, so this would have been keeping in step with that timeline. He would have had to take a San Antonio train specifically. So, what was happening in San Antonio on March 21st and 22nd of 1911? The 35th annual Convention of the Texas Cattle Raisers Association, where Governor Colquitt of Texas spoke.

More than 3,000 Cattlemen were in attendance; every hotel was filled. (*San Antonio Light and Gazette*, March 21st, 1911, pg.

1) There was also an automobile show. Being a livestock/land auctioneer and previous Buick car salesmen, I think Edward would be interested in these events. Back to Alfred Casaway, he worked as a janitor at a school and Edward liked to visit schools, he could have encountered Alfred while visiting the all-Black Grant School. Having taught school in Monroe County, Iowa where the racially diverse town of Buxton is located, engaging Casaway in a conversation would have posed no problem for Edward and possibly he was even invited to visit his home. Alfred was reported to have went to the local saloon the night of the murder and bought a bucket of beer, neither him nor his wife drank, so that's a good indication they were expecting a visitor.

The Hill Family Murders in Portland, Oregon, June 9th, 1911

William Hill (notice the initials W.H.), age 31, Ruth Cowing Hill, age 33, her two children from a previous marriage, Phillip Rintoul, age 9, and Dorothy Rintoul, age 6, were the victims of horrible rage, all were bludgeoned to death and the females were sodomized after death. This crime is different than most of the axe murders, there was theft of items from the home. I would not have included it, if it was not for the murder victim's initials, the Burris connection and the detectives Cathey Brothers.

Edward was in Villisca in the last part of May (*The Villisca Review*, May 25th, 1911). I think he is gone by June 7, because his brother Will is in Corning looking after their business interests. The Pipers have a Corning office for their auction business. (*Adams County Free Press*, June 7th, 1911, pg. 2). So, why would Edward be in Portland on June 9th? It was a direct train route from Fresno. There was a Rose Festival going on, with an electric parade that hundreds of children from the surrounding schools were participating. The Los Angeles and Portland baseball game was that day; again these are events that would interest him.

Living in Portland was past Monroe County, Iowa, residents Dr. Amos Burris and his wife Malinda Jane (Babb) Burris who lived at 439 Spokane Avenue, in the Sellwood district. Babb also was a long time family name of Albia, Iowa, and Malinda Babb probably went to school with Edward's parents Lon and Grace Ames Piper. Jessie Burris, their son, was a year younger than Edward and they would have gone to school together in Albia for a few years until both families moved away. Jessie Burris was an engineer for the Portland Railway Company and the axe victim William Hill was the representative in Sellwood of the Portland Gas and Coke plant (fancy way of saying the local plumber). He was well known in the area. I think both companies were owned by Portland Power and Light, but I could be mistaken. Another bit of information was the Hill family lived in the Sellwood district before buying the piece of land in the Ardenwald district the prior month. The house where the murders occurred was only a temporary structure (*Morning Oregonian,* June 10th, 191.1 pg. 12). In 1911, the Burris family lived in the Sellwood district approximately two miles from the Ardenwald district where the Hill family murders occurred. It is possible both Jessie and Edward killed the Hill family since it was reported two of the victims were sexually violated. I can't prove Edward was there visiting them, but the Burris name does comes up in connection with Frank F. Jones and the Moore family murders in Villisca. I find it too weird that a lot of these axe murders have people's names in common with Villisca residents or people from E.B.'s life. The name William and also the name (Hill), there is a Charles Hill who works at the Villisca National Bank; another thing in common, the Editor of the *Portland Oregonian's* name was E.B. Piper also.

The Cobles

On July 10th, 1911, young Archie Coble (A.C.), aged 25, and his bride Nettie Mae (Markel), aged 18, would be the Axeman's next victims, both were found bludgeoned to death in their little "Honeymoon" Cottage in Rainier, Washington. A young friend of Nettie Coble would find the bodies of the newlyweds still lying in bed with a sheet pulled up over their bodies. A coroner would later determine Archie's wife Nettie, as in the Hill case in Portland, was sexually assaulted after death. The authorities had four main suspects, John McQueen, a 70 year old insane farmer who was a neighbor of the Cobles; Arthur Pierce, a simple minded man who lived and worked for 15 years as a handyman in and around Rainier. Poor Arthur Pierce was literally tortured (sweated) by the sheriff to confess but he would not. (July 13th, 1911, pg. 1, *The Tacoma Times*). Swan Peterson, a 60 year old section man and hobo. He became a suspect when blood from the Coble crime was supposedly tracked to his hotel room, and finally James Wilson, a married man with five little children and an overbearing wife who actually was the one who first threw suspicion on James by claiming there was blood in his tent and Wilson's tent was 200 yards from the Coble couple's cottage. James later confessed to the murders and was convicted but had no memory of it, but was sure he was insane and did it. I think James would confess to anything to get rid of his overbearing wife and kids. Later his wife who at first was sure he did the crime would recant everything about the blood. Apparently, she was just jealous and mad at James for not kissing her and thought he was a good man and he needed to be home to take care of her and the children.

Arthur Pierce caught my attention because he was the brother of Udella Bell (Pierce) Burnham, wife of Henry Alfred Burnham (Al Burnham). Burnham was a local farmer and lumber mill owner in Rainier and later James Wilson would point the finger at an employee of the Burnham's Mill as the man who committed the crimes, but James could not remember his name just that he had been playing cards with him at the Cobles' home the night of the murders. The name Burnham ties this case to the next one in Colorado Springs in September, and the only way Edward Piper would have known anything about the Burnham name is if he had been reading the local newspaper because it wasn't nationally reported, or, he was that man playing cards at the Coble home. I wouldn't even have known if I hadn't been looking into Arthur Pierce's family and found a brief article that mentions Al Burnham's Mill in October of 1911. (*The Tacoma Times*, 14th October, 1911, Saturday, pg. 1).

The Cathey brothers were two crime scene detectives from Portland, Oregon who had previously worked on the Hill case the month before, they were absolutely positive both crimes were committed by the same individual. The Catheys were able to determined that in both cases the killer had a 31 inch walking stride and his shoe width was 3 1/2 inches and had in the past his shoe heal repaired. Edward Piper was 5 foot 11 inches and the average walking stride for a man that tall is approximately 30 inches. The Cathey brothers also said the man in both attacks was left-handed; Edward Piper was also left-handed.

The two detectives traced the blood from the Cobles attack back to the Waddell Hotel in Rainier, to room 10 where Swan Peterson had stayed that evening but left before morning as he skipped out on his lodging bill. The Catheys used a solution like luminol to see old bloodstains because there was an obvious attempt to clean up the scene at both murders and at the hotel. At the Coble's house Bloodstains were discovered by the luminol on the doorknob and bit of the towel and a Colonist Fare Folder (*The Oregon Daily Journal*, Portland Oregon, 15th July, 1911, pg. 1). I think this railroad folder is a huge clue it was dated March 10 to April 10 1911. These were daily trains from eight stops in the Midwest which offered electric light, leather upholstery seats, and tourist sleeping cars, $24one way, good for 10-day stopovers at each station en route. In my opinion, no traveling vagrant is going to be able to afford this kind of ticket. This is exactly the kind of ticket train fare Edward Piper would buy and especially since Edward, his wife and son were in Kansas City, one of the stops this fare was sold at on March 11, 1911.

The Cathey brothers also determined the killer was a tall man from the shoe prints left at the crime scenes, they also found blood on the doorknob of the hotel room and he had slept in the bed for a while and changed his clothes and stood with his hands on the back of the chair watching out the window (*The Oregon Daily Journal*, 15th, of July, 1911, pg.1 and 3).

I think Edward was possibly staying in a nearby hotel or he had seen Swan leaving early that morning and slipped into his hotel room, changed clothing and left through a window.

The Betchard family was living on a farm, also like the Burnhams, and owned a small lumber mill by Roy, Pierce County, Washington, which is 13 miles northeast of Rainier. They reported a man stopping by their farm on Tuesday the morning after the murders and discussing the Coble murders with the Betchards who knew nothing of what had happened on Monday in Rainier, because the Wednesday morning papers were the first to carry the story. The stranger asked for a meal from the Betchards, also a very Iowan thing to do. The Pierce County Sherriff, Longmire (Longmeyer name appears connected to the Paola, Kansas case) (July 18th, 1911, pg.10, *The Morning Oregonian)* was sure this was Swan Peterson because the traveler had discussed the Coble murders with the Betchard family. But when the Sherriff and the Betchards went to identify Peterson, they instantly said this is not the man who visited their farm, he was much younger, finely dressed and had a dark complexion, which also matches Edward Piper's description. (June 18th, 1911, pg. 1, *The Tacoma Times).* It was also determined that Swan's shoe size and fingerprints were not the same as the killer of the Cobles and Hill family.

Why was Edward in Washington? One of his many jobs was a land dealer and he could be possibly looking at purchasing timber land. He claimed he owned timber land by Madera, California in 1911, maybe he was curious about the sawmill business? He would later buy timber land in Louisiana in 1918-20.

The Swiss psychiatrist Carl Jung would have a field day with all the Synchronicities related between all these cases. Names and places that have no relation to one another keep popping up. It is almost like the evil that possessed a person to commit these horrific crimes had a specific plan or perhaps a train route.

The Burnham /Wayne Murders in Colorado Springs, September 17th, 1911.

These two families lived in cottages next door to one another. At 743 Harrison (notice the name of the street) Place cottage lived Henry F. Wayne (H.W.), age 30, his wife Blanche, age 26, and their two-year-old daughter Blanche. The other family at 321 West Dale Street was Mrs. Alice May Burnham, age 25, her daughter Alice, age 6, and son John, age 3. Both families were found bludgeoned to death with an axe. Mrs. Nettie Ruth, the sister of Mrs. Burnham and a Miss Merritt, a neighbor discovered the bodies; they all had been dead for several days. Miss Merritt collapsed at the sight of it all, suffering a severe heart attack, which is a bit of sensational news because Miss Merritt was just fine giving her accounts to the local newspapers. (*Salida Record,* September 22nd, 1911). Alice Burnham's husband Arthur J. Burnham (A. Burnham) was thought to be the murderer, but it was established he was at work at the Modern Woodmen Sanitarium which was located twelve miles away and he suffered from tuberculosis which left him incapable of committing the crimes. He would die the following year in 1912 of his disease.

Edward Piper arrived in Corning, Iowa from Fresno according to the newspaper on the 27th (*Adams County Free Press,* September

30th, 1911). His sister Ida May Dodd lived in Fort Morgan, Colorado and at this time was pregnant and had a young child at home. It is likely Edward would visit her and family especially since he had purchased the property and sold it to them in 1909.

Several of those Synchronicities are Mrs. Burnham's mother was named Mrs. Emma Hill; she is no relation to the Hill's that were murdered in Portland. The name Merritt occurs connected to the Showman murders; besides, there was a Burnham family in Villisca, Clyde Burnham owned a hardware store. The location of one of the murder scenes was Harrison Street; Harrison was Edward's brother Will's middle name. I think if E.B. was the killer, he had to be picking these names out of a city directory or insurance files, and not being familiar with the area went to the Wayne house by mistake or he knew the street name was Harrison and this was no mistake. The police that investigated this crime concluded the Wayne family was killed first.

Dawson Family in Monmouth, Illinois, September 30th, 1911

William Dawson (notice the name William), age 57, his wife Charity Dawson, age 52, and the youngest of their daughters, Georgia Dawson, age 12, would be all killed with a blunt object. It was the same day as a big horse sale in Villisca. The Dawsons had seven other daughters, most were grown women, three of them living at home and two of the sisters, not unlike the Stillinger girls in Villisca were spending the night with friends which would save their lives that night.

Edward had free time in Iowa from the 27th of September to October 5th when he hac an auction at Nodaway. Funny enough, it was announced on the auction bill that E.B. Piper would be there (*Adams County Free Press*, September 30th, pg. 6). He had a habit of not being where he said he was going to be, probably a good idea if your pastime is killing people. So, I checked what was going on in Monmouth, Illinois on and around the 30th. The Iowa Central Railroad was offering a special from Monmouth to Springfield and return rides for $3.50 (*Warren County Democrat,* pg. 5, September 29th, 1911). The Illinois State Fair in Springfield, opened its gate to a record crowd on Friday the 29th of September. The 59th annual Farmer Exposition started on the same day. There were motorcycle events scheduled for Friday but postponed to the 30th which had a second program. (*Chicago Livestock World,* September 30th, 1911, pg. 4). Both were events Edward would have been interested in attending.

There are some other factors in this case that could be connected to the Burnham/Wayne case and Edward. There was a flashlight found at the Dawson murder that was inscribed September 4th, 1911, Colorado Springs. I think this came from the Burnham or Wayne home because there was a Woodmen's/ Caledonian Labor Day picnic and festivities in Colorado Springs that day (*Colorado Springs Gazette,* September 4th, 1911, pg. 1). Mr. Burnham was employed at the Woodmen Sanatorium, or then again this was a big event in Colorado Springs, and it could have attracted Edward who also was a fellow Woodmen. Baseball games and a professional wrestling match between an Iowa farmer Frank Gotch from Humbolt, Iowa and a Russian George Hackenschmidt.

Frank won and was pronounced champion of the world (*Colorado Springs Gazette,* September 5th, 1911, pg. 9).

The weapon thought to be used in the murder of the Dawson family was a two-foot length of one-inch gas pipe that was found by a pond near the southbound railroad tracks. I found it interesting and maybe the killer specifically used this weapon to connect the crime to the Portland murder where the victim Mr. Hill was a pipefitter/plumber for the Portland Gas Company.

Mrs. Dawson's name was Charity Hollingsworth Dawson; Edward knew a Hollingsworth family from Monroe County, Iowa. Professor Hollingsworth was Edward's school teacher in Albia, and in same graduating class as his wife, Cora B. Sterns was Sarah Hollingsworth. I could not determine if these families were related, but then the last name might have been all it took. So, that would mean if this was part of Edward's plan, he would have had to engage a member of the Dawson family to find out this information, perhaps from one of their daughters or Edward could have stopped by the First Presbyterian Church where William Dawson was the caretaker to sell insurance. This would be easy for a man, who all his life had been engaging people whether it was selling, teaching or casual conversations.

On October the 15th, 1911, the Will (W.H.) Showman Family of Ellsworth, Kansas

The next victims would be the Showman family, William, age 31, Pauline, age 27, Lester, age 7, Fern, age 4 and Fenton, age 2. Edward was still in Iowa the first part of October and this one he about tricked me on, but I think I have figured out his movements. Edward had a court case in Red Oak around the time of the Showman family murders. The case was dismissed and E.B. settled with Mrs. Hiatt. She was the widow who Edward had sold her husband's property and kept the proceeds. (*Adams County Free Press*, October 25th, 1911, pg1). He and Will had an auction scheduled for the 18th, of October (pg. 9, *The Villisca Review*, October 12th, 1911). Then I find that Edward had been in Red Oak and Villisca on the 6th of October. This was when he could have settled the court issue in Red Oak (pg. 3, *The Villisca Review*, October 12th, 1911). (Adams County Free Press October 11th, 1911, pg. 10).

Edward's California land partner A.P. (Bert) Simpson was escorting parties to Trigo (Fresno), California on the 14th, of October. They left from Corning in the morning and picked passengers up at Villisca and Red Oak. I think Edward could have taken the train with these folks part of the way; after all, he also was trying to con them into buying that land in Trigo. (*Adams County Free Press,* October 7th, 1911 pg. 7). He could have killed the Showman family on the 15th and came back to Iowa.

Will Showman worked at the local car garage as a mechanic and as a chauffeur in Ellsworth. This was someone who it was very probable that Edward would have encountered in his numerous trips back and forth to Iowa from California. He could have known where these folks lived and could have employed Will Showman to drive him around Ellsworth.

I was left with the question, why would Edward kill the Showman family? Besides the obvious W.H. initials, I figured out what possibly took place and this is pure speculation on my part. William Showman's family were long-time citizens of Ellsworth, and it seems the Piper name was badly looked upon by the townsfolk of Ellsworth because of Zack Piper, who very well might be a relation of Edward Piper. Zack left his wife Mary and their children, and while they were still married he eloped with Nettie Barton, a daughter of a prominent Ellsworth family, and also his wife Mary's cousin. He was charged with Bigamy in Kansas, but the charge was later dismissed. Mary Piper came from a good family and was a respected and loved teacher in Ellsworth. Zack and Mary's son Robert E. Piper had changed his name to Arthur Davis after his father left him. Robert married the daughter of Civil War hero Captain Charles P. Essick of Colorado Springs who strangely enough worked for the Woodmen of the World, Pike Peak camp (had to slip in synchronicity!). In 1907, Robert along with Essick's son Paul would be accused of killing the Captain, though both were later released. But the name Piper was forever tarnished goods in the eyes of the townsfolk of Ellsworth. So, my thought is that Edward probably told Will Showman his last name and got an earful about the Pipers, and this angered Edward Piper, maybe even enough to slaughter them.

There is also the possibility that the Showman family owed a debt to someone, and sometimes people are worth more dead than alive. The Showman family also had a watchdog; the authorities thought because the dog made no sound and was locked inside, the killer must have been familiar with the Showmans and I think this could be true, but I am sure that an Iowa farm auctioneer, who had done hundreds of farm sales, had a few tricks up his sleeves when it came to dogs.

There is also another synchronicity with this murder. A few houses away from the Showmans lived Ellsworth's City Marshal Morris M. Merritt. Marshal Merritt would report someone had tried to break into his home the night of the murder, a screen to a back room window was reported cut as if to gain entry. Merritt was also the last name of one of the women that discovered the Burnham family murders in Colorado Springs. So, either these are all amazing coincidences or the killer read the newspapers or was obtaining the information about the neighborhoods from another source, and these little synchronicities were all part of his plan. I did the math. According to the 1910 Federal Census, there was a 3% chance to randomly hit a household where the head of the home was named William in Ellsworth and a 4% chance to hit a William in Monmouth by chance and in Portland, it was a .07 % chance. There were also two Arthurs and one Archie, even Henry Wayne's initials backwards is W.H. The killer had to be specifically targeting these names or initials.

There seems to be an eight-month pause in the killings, but I think this was the planning phase of the Villisca murders. Edward took out a rather sizeable weird advertisement in the Corning newspaper. It reads like a contract killer advertisement from Craigslist to me. The words in bold font are meant to stand out. **Did you know that? -Dead-I am here- lied- price**s (*Adams County Free Press*, Pg. 4, November 8th, 1911). Will (W.H.) Piper also bought that expensive property North of Villisca in December 1911 and after the fire, he could have built a new house on the

30-acre property, but I would argue he never had any intentions of staying there. And after the Moore family murders, it served him no purpose.

The Hudsons

June 1912, five days before the Moore family murders, the Hudson couple in Paola, Kansas would be killed. The Hudsons had just moved to Paola from Centerville where Rollin Hudson had been working on the Missouri-Kansas-Texas railroad (The Katy Flyer). One of the stops for The Katy Flyer was Oklahoma City; Edward Piper claimed in July that he had just been in Oklahoma previously before coming to Iowa.

Anna Hudson, the wife of Rollin, was about 21 years of age and reportedly known to be unfaithful. Maybe Edward could have been this third man? He could have met her in Centerville riding the Katy Flyer; she was close to the age he seemed to like. Maybe Anna was trying to blackmail him? By all accounts the Hudsons were fairly poor and when they were separated for a time Anna had Rollins' check garnished for living expenses. I think Edward had Bert Simpson's help with this one, either Ed was doing it for Bert and Bert was the one having an affair, or just the name Hudson could have been what sealed their fate. Serial killers don't always work alone and these men grew up together, worked and swindled people together. A.P. (Bert) Simpson was one of those "other" persons, I think might have been involved with the Villisca murder cover-up. After all, he was the son-in-law of Silas Morton, who the town Morton Mills was named after, and also where Frank F.

Jones had a branch bank. Also, Bert was in Iowa the first part of June driving his car with an unknown horse buyer (probably E.B.) around Villisca, the roads must have been bad and he left his car. He and his wife were bringing his car home to Corning on the 3rd, of June. (*Adams County Free Press*, June 5th, 1912, pg. 5).

The reason I say it's two people involved with the Hudson couple murders is a neighbor of the Hudsons who lived three doors west, Mrs. Joseph Longmeyer (Longmire is also a name from the Coble murders) had a magazine salesman come to her home on the evening of the 5th. He was flashily dressed, about 35 years old and wore a light-colored suit (Edward in 1912, was 35). When she refused him entry he got mad and left. Later that night, the same night of the murders and attempted robbery, a kimono style dress would be found in her home. It was later identified as the murder victim Anna Hudson's dress. (*Lawrence Daily Journal-World,* 7th of June, 1912 pg. 1).

About 8:30 that evening what the papers described as a swine-faced, big man and dressed in a dark suit was seen going into the Hudson's home. He also wrote down the house number before entering, and he was greeted by Anna and let in. (*Independence Reporter,* 7th of June 1912, pg.1). Mrs. Cora Pryor who lived next door reported she smelled chloroform, and she was also the one who described the swine-faced fat man at the Hudson's. (*Abilene Daily Chronicle,* 8th of June, 1912 pg. 1). To be honest, the first person I thought of was A.P. Simpson (Bert), as that is an exact description of him. A couple of days before the Moore family murders in Villisca, Iowa, the newspaper in Ottawa, Kansas printed an article stating, "It is now believed that a 'swine faced' man killed a man and wife in Paola the other day. All of the Swine Faced men that belong in Ottawa who have been traveling in the direction of Paola recently better fix up their affidavits". (*The Evening Herald*, Jun 8, 1912, Saturday, page 2). I strongly suspect whoever the killer was read the newspaper and the thought came to me that the two-pound slab of bacon wrapped in a dish cloth found by the axe at the Moore home possibly was meant to represent a "Swine Face".

After the grisly murders were discovered upon searching the Hudson's home, the authorities found scrapbooks and pictures laying out like people had been reminiscing about their past in Ohio, or family? The Hudsons were from Ohio and Bert Simpson's parents had moved to Adams County, Iowa from Ohio. But Ohio might have been enough to strike up a conversation. He could have chloroformed the Hudsons, and Edward came back later to kill them. Both men had money so obtaining chloroform would be of no difficulty, additionally I have also wondered if an opium drug was used? It seems that at a lot of the murders, food was out or prepared; I think investigating officers assumed the murderer was eating but what if that food or drink had been drugged? (Just a thought).

The kimono dress could have been a gift from this unknown lover and perhaps had a clue in it like a tag of the dressmaker being made on the West Coast or some other purpose. Edward was not always the sanest person, but I don't think he was running around in the middle of the night in Paola, Kansas wearing a dead woman's kimono dress breaking into people's homes! Mrs. Longmeyer's name fit into Edward's plan into linking this crime to the Cobles in Washington and to the Hudson couple.

Also, there is the matter of William E. Hudson (notice the initials W.H.), age 29, from Ohio, living in Villisca at the time of all these murders. Will Hudson was the manager of the Bell Phone system for three years and one year for the Mutual system. He and his (possible) mother Nancy lived with the Delaney family. He is listed on the 1910 Federal census for Villisca and is incorrectly listed as family members. Xenia Delaney would report at 2:10 a.m. on June 10th, she could hear soft footsteps coming up the stairs on the second-floor office, and she watched from her overnight cot as the doorknob slowly turned as someone was trying the locked door at the telephone office.

Will Hudson also was Villisca's Socialist Party delegate, first ward (pg. 4 of *The Villisca Review,* July 4th, 1912). So. my question is, were the killers of the Hudson family in Paola possibly trying to pin both the killings in Paola and Villisca on this William Hudson? Did William Hudson have records of who had been calling the Senator or Mrs. Albert Jones, F.F. Jones' daughter in law? Was F.F. Jones worried this information would end up in a political opponent's hands? If Edward had not dropped that Kimono dress from the Paola murder five days earlier, maybe it would have been planted at the phone office the night of Moore's murders. Will Hudson didn't stick around long, he moved from Villisca in 1913, and he and Xenia Delaney were married in 1914, in South Dakota, and both moved to Minnesota (October 14th, 1914, *The Villisca Review,* pg. 1).

Two years to the day of the Hill family murders in Oregon and one year to the day of the Moore and Stillinger murders in Villisca,

Iowa on June 10th, 1913, the Keller family would fall victims to the Axeman.

The Kellers

Arthur Ray Keller (R.K.), age 32, his wife Ida May (Ida May), age 30, and their three children, Margaret, 7, little George, age 3, and an unnamed infant lived in Harrisonville Cass County, Missouri, which is south of Kansas City about 37 miles. According to the 1910 census, Arthur was a night watchman for a local foundry but I think he must have changed jobs and started working for the railroad as a section hand, which was his job at the time of his murder.

In the early morning of the 10th of June, Ida May tapped on her neighbor Mr. Bagshaw's window calling to wake him up. He opened the door to find Ida May on his porch. She had a lantern in one hand and a bloody axe in the other. Ida said her husband had been killed and she asked Mr. Bagshaw to call Dr. Overholzer for help. When asked what the phone number was, Mrs. Keller replied she would do it herself and walked over and used his phone. She then picked up the axe and the lantern and returned to her home. About ten minutes went by and Bagshaw and another neighbor, Mrs. Kline, went over to the Keller home. They found the kitchen door unlocked and the keys sticking in the outside door lock. (I can't help but wonder if the keys were actually J.B Moore's missing house keys from the Villisca murders the year before.). The neighbor lady and Dr. Overholzer found Ida May sitting with her daughter Margaret wiping the blood from her face, she had been sleeping in her father's room when they were attacked and Arthur was lying on the bed still gasping for air. Arthur died shortly afterwards and little Margaret the next day. I think it's safe to assume Ida was showing signs of shock, not guilt.

Ida claimed the night of the attack she had lain down on a bed with her clothes on to put her younger children to sleep. Margaret had gone to bed in her husband's room, Arthur had not gone to bed yet when she fell asleep late in the night. She was awakened by a noise and she saw a man standing in the doorway between the two bedrooms, and when she arose the man had swung the axe at her and missed and then he took off running from the house. She remembered that he had a black hat on, red handkerchief tied over his face and he had brown socks on and she was able to determine that he was a white man.

When she was questioned about the brown socks, how she could determine that the man had on brown socks in low light, Ida claimed they were her husband Arthur's socks. Seems like a really bizarre thing to do, to break into a house and steal a pair of socks, oh and kill the occupants too. But the more I think about those brown socks the more I think that just like in Villisca, Edward or the killer had on moccasins. It would explain why they could not find footprints easily. I think the killer learned his lesson from the investigation the Cathey brother detectives did in Oregon and Washington, not to wear the standard men's shoes.

Ida May was arrested for the murder of Arthur and her daughter Margaret. A detective from Kansas City, Harry A. Arthur claimed to obtain a full confession from Mrs. Keller, which no one denied was under duress; he threatened her with an insane asylum and with his gun, and after two days of no sleep she confessed, but she would recant everything later. And from reading the newspaper articles I think most people believed her. But Arthur's family insisted that the couple fought regularly and this murder was about the life insurance that Arthur had that covered him and Margaret. He also was a member of Modern Woodmen of America, and had a policy with them for one thousand dollars, for both he and Margaret.

In court, Ida decried in her own defense, "Nobody loved their family better than I did." Ida May was convicted of the murders in October of 1913 and received a life sentence.

As in all the axe murder cases, there are components to the murders that are clearly connected to Edward Piper: the date of the murders, the town's name Harrisonville is connected to his brother Will Harrison, also the initials of A.R.K., Edward's brother Ralph Knox and the name of Ida May which is the same as his sister's. If anything, Ida May Keller deserves a posthumous pardon for the crime of murder.

Edward had the money to travel the trains, go to fairs, conventions and stay in fine hotels and all without drawing attention. He could be many different people if he chose to be, from a sheep farmer riding in the train car with his herd to market to a sharp dressed salesman. According to WW1 and WW2 Draft cards records, Edward was 5'11" 170 pounds, had black hair and grey eyes, a dark complexion and was of medium build. At age 35, he had been a Teacher, Principal, Auctioneer, Debt Collector, Implement Dealer, Life Insurance Salesman, Buick Car and Motorcycle Dealer, Baseball Team Manager, Land Agent for

Mexico, Canada, South Dakota and California, and an Iowa Hog & Sheep Farmer.

In truth, I cannot prove for certain that Edward, and his brother Will killed Josiah Moore's family that June night in 1912. But I feel I have more than showed they could have done the deed and their brother Ralph is probably right, they did do the deed, and I am convinced that Colonel E.B. Piper is The Axeman, one of the wickedest serial killers in U.S. history.

Made in the USA
Coppell, TX
22 October 2024